Y0-GWN-153

DELIBERATE ACCIDENT!

The foam of gray water rushed underneath with powerful speed. Though the bridge was short, the chasm below was deep and dark, and holding on to the knotted rope rail, I moved cautiously forward. Whether it was the wind that caused the bridge to shift precariously as I walked, I couldn't be sure. Then I felt something snap. Grabbing the rough edge of the bridge with both hands, I turned slowly around. The supports had given way and the bridge hung by only a thread!

There was little to keep me, and the bridge itself, from tumbling into the churning water below. Startled, I glanced back at the garden and called out in terror for help. But Charles wasn't there! I could see no one!

The horror of my position dawned on me as I made a mad leap back the way I had come. The mysterious woman had done this!

She had purposely cut the rope so that I would fall . . .

Diamond Books by Jeri Smith

THE LEGACY OF HUNTER HOUSE
WITCH TREE INN

25481491 PS
3569
M537534
W58
1992
MN

WITCH TREE INN

JERI SMITH

OCT 15 2004
DISCARDED
NORMANDALE COMMUNITY COLLEGE
LIBRARY
9700 FRANCE AVENUE SOUTH
BLOOMINGTON, MN 55431-4399

DIAMOND BOOKS, NEW YORK

WITCH TREE INN

A Diamond Book / published by arrangement with
the author

PRINTING HISTORY
Diamond edition / April 1992

All rights reserved.
Copyright © 1992 by Jeri Smith.
This book may not be reproduced in whole or in part,
by mimeograph or any other means, without permission.
For information address: The Berkley Publishing Group,
200 Madison Avenue, New York, New York 10016.

ISBN: 1-55773-689-8

Diamond Books are published by The Berkley Publishing Group,
200 Madison Avenue, New York, New York 10016.
The name "DIAMOND" and its logo are trademarks
belonging to Charter Communications, Inc.

PRINTED IN THE UNITED STATES OF AMERICA

10 9 8 7 6 5 4 3 2 1

With love to my husband

WITCH TREE INN

Chapter 1

I know exactly where to begin my story. I will start ten years ago, when I left New York City and journeyed west on the Great Northern Railroad.

My cousin Minnie, mawkish, faded beauty of the Broadway stage, was getting married. Perhaps because we were both without family—there can be no other explanation because we were never close—she came to me to talk about her fiancé.

She seemed desperately concerned, in fact almost distraught, over her relationship with her new beau, but when I queried her about the problem, she wouldn't tell me anything. Only that things could be worked out before their wedding took place that summer in a wilderness area on Lake Superior.

She insisted that it was, indeed, a shame I was so intent on starting my own dressmaking business in New York because she would adore it if I would come with her as her own private seamstress.

I stared at her a moment. "You mean come with you to Lake Superior?"

"Dear, I realize it's the end of the earth, but I thought it might be good for both of us. You can keep me company and make beautiful things, and well, as for your . . . I mean, darling, you are a divorced woman and everyone here knows that.''

''I'll go,'' I said without another thought.

And so with very little preparation and no time to worry, I found Minnie and myself traveling by railroad toward the vast Middle West.

We had journeyed west for several days under painted blue skies dotted lightly with cauliflower clouds before we turned north toward Duluth. As we neared Lake Superior, the great flatland suddenly gave way to a hillier, more rugged terrain and there was a trace of moisture in the air that betrayed water nearby.

We moved past huge thimbleberry bushes budding into summer green, riotous purple and white lilacs heavy with bloom and sweet honeysuckle; dotted along the edge of the tracks were the rich reds and blues of ripening wild fruit. A few gray clouds blew across the sun, and I shivered against the suddenly cooler air. There was a hint of cruelty in the wind. Like the elusive sun, I longed to hide and come back another day.

I felt like a coward running from New York, running from my ex-husband Clyde, but still, wasn't it justified? My life had been intolerable. I'd suffered and grieved, and longed for a different kind of life. Suddenly Clyde's ashen face rose up from the past, and his voice seemed to emanate from the clamoring train wheels, ''Another girlish fancy! You can't run from me. I'll always be there.''

Perhaps he was right. Would he always be there in the shadows, waiting for me?

''Where are you, dear?'' I glanced up at Minnie. She raised her eyebrows in a worldly woman pose and smiled thinly. I hoped she couldn't guess my thoughts. But it seemed she had.

''Look, it isn't worth brooding over. It's time you stopped feeling sorry for yourself. After all, you're the one who married the beast to begin with! And now, here we are, on the way to a wonderful new life!''

She lowered her head and whispered, "Don't you see why you married him? You were young and he was so . . . well, famous and charming. He was a matinee idol, after all! No wonder you fell for him. Poor dear, at eighteen you were so plain! And you didn't have your parents to look after you. You were lost and lonely when Clyde walked into your life! No wonder you were smitten. I wish I could give you some encouraging words, but, dear, being an actress myself, I could tell—everyone could tell—that he wasn't an actor. Once he began to age and his looks faded, he had nothing to—"

"I resent that," I said defiantly, fastening my look on her.

She leaned against the velvet seat and laughed throatily.

"My dearest Maggie, you are certainly defensive about a man you are so eager to leave!" She leaned toward me in a gesture of intimacy. "As I've said before, we create our own path in life. That's why your future is uncertain, and why I'm able to go on to a life of happiness and security." Her voice slurred on the word "security."

"Now take your Clyde . . .", she continued, but I wasn't listening. Instead I watched the ridiculous array of bright-winged beetles on Minnie's bonnet bob back and forth as she talked and picked at her unsavory lunch. Her hat was tilted forward over one eyebrow with a ridiculously high crown in the back. The rest of her costume, from the silver water-rat brooch fastened to her collar to the tortoise shell buttons of her canary-yellow and purple bodice, made me wonder how she came to have such perverse taste in dress.

And made me realize how her destiny had already decided the course my life would take. It would, fortunately, serve my purposes well that my cousin had such objectionable taste in clothes. For if she hadn't, I wouldn't have been on this train with her. Minnie was much more interested in my dressmaking skills than my happiness. And I desperately needed to leave New York.

I cut into a piece of tough beef, almost breaking my fork,

when Minnie stopped. "That's it! God's tooth, I'd expected more from the Great Northern Company! I'm going to complain."

Then there was the Scene. The waiter holding back his temper, trying to please, the head porter hovering round us and making excuses for the meal. Minnie waved her manicured hands in the air, her sapphire engagement ring flashing. I was so wretchedly embarrassed I could have disappeared under the table, yet I should have known. That was Minnie. A whirlwind of self-absorption; an upstart with no one's interest in mind but her own.

Finally, spared the cost of the seventy-five-cent meal, we settled down to our coffee. The liquid was strong and thick, but I thought it best not to complain.

"Minnie, y'know, you've hardly mentioned your fiancé this whole trip. Charles Whitney? Is that his name?"

"Darling, you know how boorish it is to talk about one's lover!" She laughed hoarsely, the sound catching in her throat. "He's rather an enigma, but, well, you'll see soon enough," she said, dismissing the subject rather abruptly.

I watched my cousin sip her coffee and wondered at her uncharacteristically odd behavior. Minnie was seldom secretive, especially about a new conquest. I stared out the window at the gathering gloom, trying to fathom why she hadn't shown me a photograph of him, described his manner, told me how much money he made. . . .

"Darling dear, you have the disturbing habit of not listening! I'm asking you if you want to try on my engagement ring. Here, let me see, I'll bet it fits!"

Minnie's eyes were bright with a feverish excitement, her voice a little too loud.

"Isn't it bad luck to try on a ring before the wedding?" I smiled.

"Oh, fiddlesticks! Go on, don't be a bore."

I slipped it on the third finger of my left hand. The deep azure crystal sparkled richly in the fading light. Aha! I mused. Her trophy! Poor fool that waited for such a capricious woman!

I forced enthusiasm. "It's lovely, Minnie. It really is."

"Wear it for a while! It becomes you. You could really be stunning if you started wearing jewelry and stopped dressing in wren's brown all the time! You design dresses, for goodness sakes, make something a little more . . . appealing."

"I suppose I should."

"You really have a lovely face, y' know! China-white skin that most women would die for, round, almond eyes, full lips. Maggie, if you wore makeup and gowns with a little style, you could be beautiful!"

"Surely you realize my financial situation, if anyone does! How can I purchase French silk brocades when I can hardly feed myself?" My voice was full of exasperation.

In the distance, beyond the hum of conversation and clacking wheels, there came a rumble of thunder. A voice filtered through the crowded car. "They've had lots of rain hereabouts, some trouble with the tracks . . ."

"Well, now you can! When you order material for me, you can buy extra for yourself. We'll be the best-dressed ladies this side of the . . . what's the name of that big river out here? The Missouri?"

"Mississippi."

"Oh, yes. God, what a long way from civilization!" She pouted and looked out the window. Then, surprisingly, she took off her hat.

She looked mournfully at the cone of beetle wings and velvet and lace. "I hope we can use these pretty clothes here." She glanced up at me. "Imagine. Me! Waiting all this time to marry, and now I've got to live—"

The train jerked spasmodically, shaking us both. I heard a woman's gasp and the rumble of complaints. The coffee cup halfway to Minnie's mouth shook and spilled its contents onto the hat she held on her lap.

"Damn!" she cursed. "This is the most despicable train

trip I've ever been on! They advertised having special springs to keep the ride smooth."

"Oh, for God's sake, Minnie, not all bumps can be helped. They probably hit an unlevel place in the ground or something."

"Unlevel, my aunt! Listen, dear, look at this toque!"

She was furiously dabbing at the ornamental contraption with water, sighing impatiently as she worked. I leaned over the table and could see that the lace was hopelessly stained.

In a halfhearted gesture, I removed my own hat. It was impossibly plain, but it was fashionable, nonetheless.

"Here, Minnie, you can borrow mine if you like. I'm sure when we arrive you can have someone clean your hat for you. And I don't mind. Really."

She glanced appraisingly at my hat and slanted a look at me.

"I think not, but, dear, would you be an angel and go back to my sleeping compartment to fetch me another of my own? There's a lovely little lavender one in my trunk. I think it will go nicely." She smiled pleadingly.

I shot her a look of derision. The tedium of the long journey had taken its toll, and now I was running at her beck and call. She would have to think again if she thought of me as her personal maid.

But, for the moment, there was nothing for it but to comply with her suggestion.

"All right. I guess I'll have to." I stood.

"Good! Don't look so glum, dear. It will only take a moment. Here, let me watch your handbag for you. You can't be too careful of pickpockets! And while you're away, I'll order sherry. Now, if only I can find the key to my trunk. . . . Damn these enormous traveling bags!"

She was rummaging through her purse when I was practically knocked off my feet by a tobacco-chewing gentleman who was having difficulty negotiating the narrow aisle. I was forced to back away, so Minnie thrust her handbag at me.

"Darling, the key is in there somewhere. . . ."

I grabbed her bag and made my way through the dining car, hurrying back along the narrow, half-empty compartments.

It took little time to get to Minnie's Pullman at the back of the train. And, after digging through Minnie's handbag for several moments, I reached into the inside cashmere pocket. I pulled out several calling cards—and the keys to her trunk. I unlocked the trunk and began searching through her brocades, silks and satins. I finally found her hat boxes stowed in the bottom.

Pulling the lavender toque from its tissue wrapping, I noted that it was nothing more than a piece of velvet with an orchid feather attached. I locked the trunk and, returning the key to her purse, gazed out at the soft rain that had begun to fall. I began thinking of what to do as her dressmaker—after all, our journey was almost at an end. It was my good fortune that we could use the same pattern. We were almost identical in size and stature.

Mercifully, our styles and manners were exceedingly different. And I could easily tailor our attire to fit our unique personalities.

Holding the hat carefully so that I would not crush it, I shook aside my reverie and began walking up toward the door of the Pullman. There was a sudden loud cracking noise, and I was hurled forward upon the velvet seat, wrenching my arm. Something must be wrong! I thought, dazed.

As I stood, regaining my equilibrium, the wheels screeched shrilly, and we slammed into—I later learned—a flood of water. My last recollection was grabbing at the tassel trim on the plush hanging in the doorway. I don't remember if the brass railing came tumbling down on my head, but something hit me hard, and I was knocked unconscious.

It must have been mere moments that I lay there. Trying to sit up made a fist of nausea rise in my throat, so I reclined again. My head felt as though it was split open, but when I touched it, tenderly, there was no blood.

It wasn't long before there were shouts and the sound of blunt instruments trying to pry open the jammed doors of the train. Suddenly the door on Minnie's car opened with a crash, and I watched distantly, as though looking through a murky haze.

A man wearing work clothes jumped onto the car and moved carefully toward me. "Can you move?" he asked calmly, glancing quickly toward the open trunk.

"Yes, I think so, but . . . my head."

"Let me carry you." With economy of movement, he lifted me effortlessly into his arms.

There was no time to see his face, but cradled close to him I caught a glimpse of his jawline. It was set tight, the shadow of a day's beard covering it. A vein in his neck rose, beat for a moment, then disappeared. He never turned or looked down at me.

Yet there was something intimate about the way he held me. His hard arms under my back were as solid as steel, and unbearably gentle. As he jumped down from the train and we moved, rescuer and victim, out into the inclement weather, he tightened his grip slightly. For the first time in many years I felt safe.

He never asked how I felt or tried to soothe me. And, somehow, it didn't matter. I was at his mercy, and I clung round his neck as we ran for cover toward a waiting carriage.

He handed me inside the warm conveyance, and as he closed the door, I heard him giving orders to the driver. Before the trap lurched forward, I glanced out the rain-splattered window. But I couldn't see him. He'd already gone.

Chapter 2

It was hard to tell where we were headed. A rainy fog surrounded us as we drove over a rutted, muddy path, through a two-horse town, finally pulling up to a rambling stone mansion set well back from the road. The driver jumped down from his box and came round for me. As he opened the door, he offered an umbrella.

I took it gratefully and let him help me up the stone steps to the front entrance. The pain in my head was so great at this point that I don't recall with any accuracy the order of the things that followed.

I do remember being taken up a flight of winding stairs to a large, airy room. I was laid on a bed so soft that I sank into it. Through a roaring mist I recall someone undressing me, letting out my stays, taking off my stockings, helping me into a rather coarse nightdress. The lights were dimmed, and I was given some nasty-tasting medicine that made me sleep. It seemed years before I awoke. In reality, it was only a few hours.

The room was stuffy, and as I stirred, the weight of heavy blankets clung to me. Three distinct voices spoke in funereal tones, and there was the sound of someone dipping into water. I felt a warm compress touch my forehead, and pulling out of a swirling cloud of unconsciousness, I looked around. A flickering gaslight burned, and I closed my eyes again against the sharp pain.

"Madam! Madam! She looked at me, I swear. Her eyes opened!" a female voice rang out. It had a distinct Irish lilt.

"Now, now, Miss Rose, we must be calm," a dreary-sounding man's voice replied. "We can't agitate her any more. She's had a terrible shock to the nervous system."

"Dr. Clemens, will she be all right?" This new voice was that of an older woman, and it held an unmistakable tone of severity.

"It seems so. From what I can tell about her physical condition, she has escaped completely unscathed. But about her psychic condition, of that, I cannot be sure."

"Miss Dallworth's a beautiful girl, ain't she, Doctor? If she recovers, she'll be marrying Mr. Whitney next week." It was the Irish voice again.

I opened my eyes a second time. Glints of light reflecting off polished articles dazzled me, and I held my head a moment.

"Miss, Miss . . . can you see me?" A craggy, oval face wearing a monocle peered at me. "My name is Dr. Clemens, and I've been attending you. How do you feel?"

The lights dulled a bit, and the room began to come into focus. My head still hurt, but it was a duller pain.

"I . . . I don't know," I mumbled foolishly.

"Of course she doesn't. She's suffered a terrible strain. And it's probably upsetting her to wake up to a room full of strangers asking questions. Thank the good Lord she's alive! Rose, that will be all."

I was grateful for the elderly woman's solicitous remarks, and when I whispered a hoarse "thank you," I got a better look at her. She was immense in size, with a great frontage of white teeth and a grim red face fastened right onto thick-set shoulders. I looked away and felt tears sting my eyes.

It was overwhelming. My leaving New York, the journey, the accident, and now landing here, in God know's where.

"Where am I?" I turned to face them.

"Well, humm, you're at the Witch Tree Inn, madam," Dr. Clemens answered me after a moment.

"Witch Tree Inn?" I asked incredulously.

"Your final destination. In Duluth. It's an *inn*, dear. Named after an old cedar standing on a spit of rock over Lake Superior. Just through the woods apiece. Don't be afraid, child. You're at the right place."

I sighed audibly.

The huge woman with hard, round eyes went on. "You must be a woman of the church; it's obvious you have faith in the Almighty. You've arrived in good health so you could be blessed with marrying Mr. Whitney."

"What do you mean, marry?" I tried pulling myself up.

The doctor gave me a pitying glance and said, "Your fiancé. Surely you haven't forgotten that Mr. Whitney is the man you are to marry?"

"No, no, dear. You're too weak," the woman said levelly. "Don't try to get up. All in good time. All in good time." She bustled around to the end of my bed, tucking in the blankets.

"Let her lean against the pillows at least. Surely that can't harm her?" the doctor pleaded, rather than stated.

"All right, but easy does it." With their assistance, I was brought up to a sitting position. A whirling dizziness engulfed me for a moment, then the room came back into focus again.

My eyes lit on the fine appointments surrounding me. The tasteful peach chintz wallpaper, a crackling fire in the grate, twin wall sconces above the carved overmantel and matching walnut dresser and marble table. The table was set with tea and biscuits and a pewter vase with extraordinary lilacs in hues of purple, their intoxicating smell wafting through the room. The carpets had leaf patterns of rose, peach and blue, and tossed carelessly on a velvet armchair . . . could it truly be Minnie's hat?

I swallowed hard. "Where is she?"

A questioning look passed between them and neither spoke.

"Who dear?" The doctor was paternally patting my hand.

"Minnie, of course. Is she all right?"

Again that concerned look. It was almost one of suspicion.

"Darling, you've had a terrible shock. It's plain to see. Are you feeling hungry at all? We have some lovely tea biscuits." The woman's button eyes surveyed me closely.

"I want to see her!" My tone was definitely harsh.

The doctor, plainly perturbed at my insistence, took the woman aside, and they walked some distance from me. He glanced back at me only once during their conversation and gave me a look of open concern. After a few moments, they returned to my bedside.

"Don't worry, dear." She took my hand in her fat paw and held it there. "You're suffering a sort of amnesia! In a day or two—"

"It can be longer, Mrs. Svenson."

The doctor fixed a look on me. "Miss Dallsworth, a loss of memory can occur after a great shock such as you've just had. It's no surprise to me that you think you are someone else."

"Wait a minute." I pulled my hand away, and held both hands up as a sign of surrender. "Do you think *I'm* Minnie, and I've just forgotten who I am?"

Mrs. Svenson, as the doctor called her, pulled in her chin and stared at me.

"Dear, you *are* Miss Dallsworth. But you mustn't worry about all this now. You have to be quiet." She turned to Dr. Clemens. "Well, Doctor. How soon will it pass?"

"It can take time, Mrs. Svenson. And we've certainly got

that. Time. Let her rest, and eat to regain her strength, and she'll be back to normal in a few days."

"But listen to me." My trembling voice faltered painfully. The sharpness of the moment blurred for me, and I could say nothing more. They eyed me oddly.

"Miss Dallsworth, you're looking ill again. Why don't you lie back and try to get some more sleep?" That from the doctor.

"Sleep! How can you be so absurd?"

There was a painfully long pause. I caught the glance Mrs. Svenson gave the doctor and knew at once how completely disbelieving they were.

"Surely you can't think . . . look, my name is Magdela Mansfield. I'm . . . I've come as Minnie's dressmaker." I looked from one impassive face to the other.

"This is preposterous. It sounds like black magic or something! How can you think I'm Minnie when . . ." My voice trailing off, I noted the dancing shadows high on the wall caused by the snapping fire. Ghoulish shadows played over the hovering faces before me, and I felt I had surely gone mad.

My heart hammered wildly against my chest, and when I covered my face to hide from their scrutiny, my fingers felt wet and clammy.

"There's nothing more can be done for you," came Mrs. Svenson's rigid voice.

I pulled my hands away and looked at the old man and matron for a wavering moment. Clearing my throat, I managed to speak steadily enough. "I know Minnie and I have the same hair and eye color, but we don't look alike! Our voices are different, we move differently, we think differently. I design clothes, I create fashions from my own patterns. Minnie has terrible taste in dress! Why do you think she'd wear something like this—"

I stopped short. I was garbed in a cotton nightgown, and when I made a quick survey of the room, my glance lit on my teal gown thrown carelessly over a velvet settee. My

God! I thought, why should I try to explain our different taste in clothes? It was obvious that no one here even *knew* Minnie! These people had no idea that Minnie wouldn't wear a gown like mine.

Her ring! I remembered, looking down. It was there alright—on the third finger of my left hand. And if this weren't enough, I'd been found in Minnie's private Pullman. No wonder everyone thought I was Minnie. . . .

They must have seen some sort of understanding dawning, incredulously, on my face, but I said nothing. Nor did they. The irrational feeling that they had to believe me persisted, however.

I drew in a sharp breath and tried to speak. "Surely there's something, some way of identifying me. Someone who'll know I'm not Minnie. There must be a way to prove who she is, who I am!"

There was another weighty silence. Mrs. Svenson pulled at her coils of rag curls; the doctor cleared his throat.

"There is, of course, Mr. Whitney," the doctor stated evenly.

"Yes, yes!" I said breathlessly. "That's it. Charles Whitney. Surely he'll know I'm not Minnie. Surely he'll know his own fianceé!" I tried to laugh, but it came out in a short staccato burst.

"I suppose we should try it?" It was a question posed at Mrs. Svenson, who suddenly took on an attitude of open defiance.

"Dr. Clemens," her words were curt and short, "this is absurd and improper. I don't think Mr. Whitney should be brought in to identify his own betrothed! After all, he's the one who saved—"

"On the contrary, Mrs. Svenson, I'd be pleased to identify Miss Dallsworth."

It was a voice of authority, causing Mrs. Svenson and the doctor to jump simultaneously. They stared at the figure in the doorway with burgeoning resentment.

"The young lady's had a shock," came the doctor's stuttering response.

"Mr. Whitney," Mrs. Svenson tightened her lips and gestured toward him. "It's not proper to be dressed so casually, and in a woman's bedroom!"

"You'll all pardon my attire," he said in a rich, sonorous voice as he came closer to me.

But not until Mrs. Svenson and the doctor stepped obligingly away from the bedside did I see him.

I hadn't meant to stare, but he awakened a feeling of safety in me I'd felt only once before—earlier that day. His was a shattering presence. He seemed to exude an energy that illuminated the room. Yet as my glance swiftly touched on his clothes, from his mud-splattered Hessian boots to his soiled trousers and collarless shirt, it was obvious they did little to disguise his physical appeal. His lean body of straight lines and hard angles was arrogant in its perfection, yet his tanned forearms and sinewy hands looked gentle, even in their ruggedness.

His unruly toast-colored hair was unstylishly long; his mustache unkempt; his contemptuous mouth closed tightly. As his steel-gray eyes met mine across the expanse of room, I saw the glint of mischief there, and the severity.

It was impossible to speak—or even to draw breath. I do remember placing a cool hand on one cheek, but I forced myself to match his riveting look stare for stare. Now I knew who had rescued me from the train.

Then he laughed. It wasn't malicious or cynical. It was a marvelous, catching sound, and I smiled in spite of myself.

There was a stirring in the corner as the doctor came forward, and I remember how pathetic Dr. Clemens looked as he stood next to this man.

"Tell us, Mr. Whitney, you obviously know, is this your betrothed? Is this Minnie Dallsworth?"

The laughter died in Mr. Whitney's throat, and he looked calmly at Dr. Clemens. "Is there some sort of problem here?"

"Yes, you see, she claims to be someone else, but, of course, she's suffered a great strain to the system." The doctor fidgeted nervously.

"So, if you'd be so kind, Mr. Whitney." Mrs. Svenson's voice was an octave higher than it had been, her movements sharper, more agitated. "The good Lord brought her to you, so if you'd just tell us that this young lady is, indeed, Miss Dallsworth, then I can begin on preparations for the wedding."

As I watched the scene before me, I felt my breathing return to normal. "Mr. Whitney," I said, as the granite look settled on me once more, "please tell them that I am not your betrothed! It's obviously a case of mistaken identity. My name is Magdela Mansfield. I'm Minnie's cousin, as you must see."

His eyes darkened dangerously and he walked swiftly to my bedside with a fluid, lazy expertness of movement. Coming close he gazed at me boldly, taking one of my trembling hands in his.

"My darling, the doctor's right. You've had a great shock, and now you must rest. I don't know why we should all be so concerned. A traumatic shock like this is common after so devastating an accident. Sleep, dear, because next week we will be married."

A roaring dizziness engulfed me again as I whispered, "No!"

Mr. Whitney pulled his hand away and turned sharply to the waiting doctor and Mrs. Svenson. "She'll be back to herself again soon, I assure you. I trust both of you to take good care of her."

There was no sound in the vast bedroom as he strode easily toward the door. No one moved except Mr. Whitney. He reached the door and, placing a hand on the doorknob, turned to me. There was no glint of laughter in his eyes as he bowed slightly and whispered under his breath, "Minnie." With that, he was gone.

I swallowed hard, trying to make sense of what had

happened. It was only a moment until the doctor and matron began bustling about me once more, trying to make me comfortable. Through the flurry of activity, I managed a query.

"Was . . . anyone killed?"

"My dear! That's not an appropriate question right now," came Mrs. Svenson's tart reply.

The doctor let down his guard, ignoring Mrs. Svenson's comment. He rubbed my arm gently as if to ward off pain and spoke quietly.

"It was a very severe accident. The dining car was right behind the locomotive. The first cars were almost completely destroyed. You see, when the train came roaring around the corner, the engineers didn't have time to brake before they hit the flood of water covering the tracks."

"Water?"

"Child, it's an unusual phenomenon, but in the spring up here beavers build their dams. During that time, Otter Creek backs up and damages the railroad bed lying right next to it. There was several feet of water covering the tracks. When the train hit it . . . in simple terms, Miss Dallsworth, the dining car derailed going at a tremendous speed."

"You must thank the good Lord that you were safe in your Pullman," Mrs. Svenson stated tonelessly. "That car was hardly touched since it was at the back of the train."

I gave a sudden gasp. "Minnie! I left her in the dining car." I grabbed the doctor's sleeve savagely.

"We don't know all the facts yet," the doctor said quietly, his hand covering mine.

"The police are still busy. No one knows how many passengers were injured . . . or died." Mrs. Svenson crossed heavy arms over her square chest and stared down at me.

"I see," I answered hoarsely and, falling back onto the bed, burst into tears.

It was bad luck for both of them that I seemed so inconsolable. Mrs. Svenson tried to get me to eat, murmuring platitudes on suffering, and the doctor stayed next to me, his eyebrows knit with concern. After a few moments he wrapped a thin, but surprisingly strong, arm around me.

"I suppose I must try to sleep, but this all seems so unreal!" I finally managed in a cracked, breathless voice.

"It's plain to see that she hasn't grasped the situation yet." Mrs. Svenson's tone was ingratiating.

The doctor merely shook his head and poured some amber-colored liquid from a cut-glass decanter. "Here, Miss Dallsworth, drink this."

I drank obediently and gasped as I swallowed the burning tonic.

"Don't worry, you'll feel relaxed soon," the doctor said as I handed him my empty glass.

"I suppose so," I answered drearily. The doctor held my hand warmly, and he and Mrs. Svenson began talking endlessly about nothing at all. It was an obvious effort to make me forget and possibly to sleep.

It worked. Before long I gave in to a nagging weariness and closed my eyes. I didn't sleep right away, though, and heard the doctor and matron whispering a moment before they pulled the bedroom door closed with a soft click.

I slept feverishly after that. It is hard to tell how long I slumbered, but after a time I awoke abruptly for no apparent reason.

I sat up in bed and tried to fathom why I had awakened. Perhaps it was the sound of the wind through the trees, or was that a surf that I heard? On the table next to my bed a lamp burned low, casting a circle of lemony light on me. I reached for it and turned the cock. The pool of light widened and sent the menacing shadows to the edges of the room.

I put my feet on the floor and, holding the lamp in one hand, stood and made for the windows. Heavy brocade curtains were pulled tightly across them, but I knew instinctively that it wasn't light yet.

I felt strangely lightheaded and my legs were weak, but my brain seemed to function surprisingly well. When I got to the windows, I found a tasseled cord and pulled the paneled drape open. Peering through the glass curtains, my eyes lit on the crashing surf against a rocky shore!

A full moon hung high in the black sky, casting its metallic light on the jagged shoreline. Water shot up, as if from some invisible fountain, and exploded in a spray of foam in the air above.

Fog clung around the ground in patches, and suddenly a filmy cloud rose before me, blocking my vision. I tried to peer through the mist when a shadowy specter materialized threateningly in front of me. I choked and wheeled back, almost dropping the lamp.

It was Clyde! In a blink, he was gone. I told myself it was only an odd trick of light and shadow created out of the eerie lake air.

Yet the manifestation of his severe face stirred in me that old dread and loathing I wanted so much to forget. Memories of that unhappy married woman I once was sprang to mind again. And brought me reeling back to the reality of my situation—a young, newly divorced woman, entirely alone and without a prospect for the future.

Damn him! I cursed, for reminding me of all this unpleasantness. With mounting resentment, I ran back to the security of my bed and crawled under the covers. Had my agitated subconscience drummed up his angry face as a sort of warning? Was he, indeed, following me at this very moment to the edge of civilization where I'd hoped to be safe?

It would be like Clyde to do that—if only to get revenge. Yet it seemed highly improbable that he could find me here. My former landlady didn't know where I'd gone, no one in New York knew that I had followed my cousin. Still . . .

Why had Mr. Whitney identified me as Minnie? Was it possible that *he* had never seen her before? Whatever grim plan I was unwittingly involved in, I had to be very careful.

But a fearful scheme kept hovering around the edge of my consciousness, though I tried to push it away. What if I stopped resisting? Stopped pleading that I was, indeed, Maggie? What if I went along with this treacherous deception . . . ?

No one here knew the difference. It was quite obvious that none of the servants had ever seen Minnie's photograph—or knew anything about her. Including, I thought with horror, her own fiancé!

But . . . what about Minnie? Was she really dead? Perhaps she was still alive and had been mis-identified, too. If she is alive, there is no turning back, I thought morbidly—even if they eventually discover who I am. Meanwhile . . . meanwhile I will be known as Minnie Dallsworth!

I knew then what Minnie would do if she could hear me. She would throw back her head and laugh deviously. "You're mad as a hatter!" She'd say, but she would enjoy the joke.

However, this was no joke. It was a grim, dangerous and, yes, intriguing reality.

A strange euphoria swept over me as I thought of the possibilities. Hadn't Minnie mentioned she'd be rich? Wouldn't it be easy to claim I was her . . . after all? As the sound of the crashing water below answered "yesssss, yesssss," I fell into a heavy, dreamless slumber.

Chapter 3

When I awoke the next morning it was broad daylight. The room that had seemed diabolical the night before now took on a cheery, bright personality. Sun streamed through the open window and reflected off the gleaming wood surfaces. It shone on a delicate-looking woman pouring coffee. I took a gulp of warm, moist air, and as I stretched, there came the plaintive cry of a seagull calling from the sill.

"Oh! M'lady Dallsworth! I was hopin' yer'd wake soon. Would ye like some coffee?" I recognized the musical Irish lilt as the one I had heard last night, before Mrs. Svenson had dismissed the woman.

"Thank you." I accepted the cup gratefully and sipped the aromatic liquid slowly. It seemed I hadn't tasted anything so good in years. "You must be Rose," I stated as the maid began sweeping out the cold grate.

I was surprised to note that she was much older than myself; the hair under her mobcap was gray and her hands were lined. I felt a pang of pity for her. She turned to me and dropped to a formal curtsey.

"Sorry, m'lady, don' know what's come over me. Yes, that's me name. How'd you know?"

"Oh, a little bird told me," I winked toward the seagull on the sill. "What time is it, anyway?"

"It's near one o'clock, m'lady. Hope y'er feelin' better. Doctor'll be in any minute. 'Fraid he's got some bad news." She turned back to me, wiping her hands on her crisp, white apron. "The train wreck. It was worse than they thought at the beginning, and some bodies was identified."

I winced at her words, and suddenly my head began to ache again. I massaged my temples a moment, contemplating the situation.

I smiled feebly. "I was hoping not to be exposed to anything more stressful than breakfast right now!"

Rose merely smiled apologetically and went back to her work.

There was not much time to indulge in my first cup of coffee, for after a moment or two the fumbling doctor was upon me, asking if I felt strong enough for some "pretty awful news." I, in turn, nodded that I could handle any sort of news—that, indeed, I was prepared.

Biting my lip, I listened to the doctor's dreary account of what had happened only yesterday. Though the news he imparted was devastating, his voice was so dull and he spoke in such low tones, I could only think of my rumbling stomach. When he finally reached the end of his account, his words struck me, and I felt the blood drain from my face.

". . . And when they found her, well, it was obviously your poor cousin. Mr. Whitney informed us that you were traveling with your cousin, Magdela Mansfield, and that she was hired as your private dressmaker. Her traveling handbag was found next to her, and all her personal effects were inside, including a locket with her mother's photograph, or rather . . . your aunt's."

I drew in a sharp breath and gasped. I tried to speak, but my words sank and I merely coughed.

"I'm very sorry, Miss Dallsworth. We didn't know yesterday what we know now. The train has been thoroughly searched, the bodies taken away to the mortuary."

I stared at the doctor in stunned silence.

"I will spare you the awful procedure of identifying your cousin. She will be properly taken care of, the funeral arrangements dealt with. You must rest and drink plenty of milk and cream."

He held a topper in one hand and he passed his other hand across his drawn face. He pulled a chain with his monocle dangling on the end from his vest pocket. Setting the glass in his eye, he proceeded to examine me.

I said nothing and sat obediently as he checked my respiration, my throat, my ears, my eyes. He placed a cool hand on my temple and felt my wrist for pulse.

Smiling paternally, he stroked my hand and asked, "Dear, dear, how are you feeling?"

"I feel better today, yet the shock of all this . . ." I mumbled.

"Of course. Your response is quite normal."

"Doctor," my voice sounded oddly shrill, "please, it would help if I could move around. Leave my chambers. I need to get some fresh air. Please, may I?"

He agreed that I was ready if, he stated anxiously, I wasn't feeling any more memory loss. I could leave my room only if I was back to my old self again.

I could have argued again that my old self wasn't really Minnie, that I, Magdela Mansfield, felt good as new. But I didn't. Taking my first decisive step in the novel role I'd chosen to play, I smiled nervously and agreed that, yes, I was feeling fine.

"Then it's all settled. You may move around the inn as long as you're not too tired. Take your meals in the dining room if you wish, get acquainted with your new home, but if you venture outside, dress warmly. Though the weather is mild now, it can change at any moment. If you"—he gave me a long look, and I wondered, for a startling moment, if he was on to me—"catch a chill, it would be most undesirable, and possibly dangerous to your health."

"Very well. I promise to obey your instructions," I replied almost glibly.

The doctor smiled his approval and left instructions for Rosa to fetch my lunch, which I accepted more than gratefully, and soon I was alone.

After taking my time bathing, brushing and plaiting my hair and then dressing in my soiled teal silk gown again, I felt a smug satisfaction creep into my bones.

I forced a smile and set my shoulders. I knew then there was no going back. If the benign hand of fate had brought me here, it was now a freak twist of fate that had brought about my role of imposter. For here I was in the heart of an unexplored wilderness, expected to marry a man I'd never seen before. A man who would now dictate my future, whether I liked it or not.

Who was he, really? Either he was an imposter himself or he was hiding something. His insolence was so intimidating, his figure so imposing, that I feared he could only be dangerous. And yet he had a certain quality, a sort of gentleness incongruous to what he seemed to be. Whoever he was, he piqued my interest more than I cared to admit.

The weather outside beckoned me, so I decided to push aside my growing alarm and take a peek outside. I discovered that I had no cape to wear, but decided that the day seemed much too balmy to need one anyway. Making for the door, I almost stumbled into Mrs. Svenson.

She stood solidly in the doorway, wearing a dress of deep orange which did not compliment her ruddy complexion. Her sleeves were short, exposing fleshy arms, and the bow-trimmed bustle was a fanciful attempt at looking younger. She greeted me warmly, but beneath her obsequious tone, I detected contempt.

"I thought it wise to have your clothes—and those of your dear, deceased cousin—brought up to you. Will it be convenient for us to bring them to you right now?"

I told her that I was leaving to take a stroll but that having my own wardrobe back sounded heavenly. The dress I wore was stiff from having been soaked and there were mud splatters on the bodice.

"It will only take a few moments to bring you your belongings, then you are free to go."

With my acquiescence, she moved out of the room quickly, and I couldn't help notice that despite her size she moved with grace, her shoulders and head held high.

Only a few moments passed before she returned with a thin, frail-looking boy, in navy livery, hefting Minnie's huge trunk, my portmanteau and both our framed handbags. She ordered him here and there, and it pained me to note that he had such an intense desire to please he actually trembled.

"Dear," she accousted me after dismissing the eager boy. "I haven't properly introduced myself. My name is Mrs. Svenson, and I've been asked by Mr. Whitney to oversee the running of things, since . . . well, he has only just purchased the inn, you know. There was no way of knowing how smoothly everything would go. I mean with your arrival and all."

"I see," I answered flatly.

"I daresay your color is better, if you don't mind. And you are a lovely young lady, but don't you think perhaps the gown is a bit . . . I mean, the bodice is rather mud-splattered, don't you agree?" She scrutinized me closely.

I smiled condescendingly. "You may be right. But I'm afraid that it's all I had to dress in before my luggage arrived."

"Oh, of course!" She clapped her hands gleefully as if she had triumphed over sin.

"I'll leave you to unpack, then."

"Yes, I'd appreciate it," I agreed rather quickly.

"Oh, by the by," she said in dulcet tones, "I'm a widow, so I understand death and grief. If there's anything you need, anything at all, I want you to come to me."

"Thank you," I replied dully.

"I'm sure you read the Bible and take heart from that, but I'm a member of a wonderful Lutheran church, and I'd be proud to take you with me sometime to meet the congregation. And the pastor—bless his soul—is such a kind man!"

I was distractedly playing with a covered button on my bodice. "Yes, I'd like that," I told her, but I hoped to find an excuse not to go.

"I've already arranged with the pastor to have him preside over the funeral ceremony. He recommends you come to hear his sermon on death. Would that suit you?" She was peering at me closely, her round blueberry eyes bright with excitement.

"That would be just fine, but if you'll excuse me—"

"Oh, of course, you must get settled. I'll leave you to your task then." She hurried away, her plump body proud and erect, pulling the door closed behind her.

Slowly I picked up Minnie's fawn leather purse, opening the clasp. Was there a clue here that would help me understand what was happening?

Inside there was the typical miscellany of a woman's traveling handbag: a silver comb, embroidered handkerchiefs, lace gloves, a leather wallet, the inside cashmere pocket that held calling cards and keys. I had seen all this before when I'd searched it for the key to her trunk.

I pulled out the wallet and turned it over in my hand. Several dollars and some change fell into my palm. Nothing startling or out of the ordinary in her purse. Perhaps there was something in her luggage that I had missed. . . .

I removed the keys and went quickly to Minnie's great black box. With a strange distaste, I turned the key and unlocked the trunk for the second time. Shimmering material, feathers, velvets and lengths of lace lay before me, tucked and folded and ready to hang in a wardrobe.

It was too overwhelming to search through her belongings in hopes of finding some clue. Instead I grabbed my portmanteau, and finding a saffron walking suit, changed clothes quickly. I found a simple, conical-shaped hat in matching yellow and placed that on my head. I made for the door once again.

As I went down the endlessly long shadowy hall, the closed paneled doors that lined the walls seemed to mock me. Soft halos of flickering light shimmered in their gas globes, and my skirts brushed silently along the thick carpets. With my shadow following me, I descended the surprisingly narrow, curving stairway to the gallery entrance below.

As I made my way toward the front door, I noted the tasteful but simple decor. The floors were shiny parquet partially covered with Oriental rugs in deep earth tones. Widespread ferns were placed against the walls in odd juxtaposition to the walnut chairs next to them. A graceful cabinet with inlaid ivory stood close to the entrance next to the untended oak front desk. I was glad that there was no concierge to greet me.

I slipped unnoticed out the front door. Emerging into the late afternoon sunlight, I shielded my eyes against the red-orange glare. As my eyes adjusted, I inhaled deeply, taking in all the smells of warm summer greenery.

A terrace of green velvet stretched out before me, and I descended the stone steps to the grass. Immense pine trees bordered the lawn and filled the air with their fragrance. Large, stately elms and oaks stood tall and majestic, their leafy branches intermingled in a sort of vaulted archway above my head.

As I crossed the lawn, I heard the lonely whisper of wind through the trees, and my heart lurched at the sorrowful sound. Crossing my arms protectively over my chest, I stared back at the inn. It was enormous. Built in Tudor style, it was a monstrosity of stone and wood beams. A curl of smoke rose from one of its chimneys toward a sky that trembled on the brink of dusk.

There was a drive, I noticed, that wound away from the inn and seemed to lead toward a main road. I decided to follow it. Beech trees lined the winding, muddy path, and wild mushrooms, plants thick with scarlet berries and patches of emerald moss all thrust themselves out of the moist summer earth.

If there is such a town as Duluth, I mused, it is either quite a distance away or it consists of nothing more than the inn and, quite probably, a post office. Smiling, I squatted down to pluck up one of the shiny berries when the ground shook and a sound like thunder echoed through the trees. I stood quickly.

An enormous chestnut-brown horse came pounding down the path, its rider leaning slightly forward toward its head. They came straight at me, the canopy of leaves overhead melting away from them as they sped along. I swayed back as powerful man and beast stopped, abruptly, just short of me. Clutching my berries in one hand, I grasped a sapling tree with my other. I was not a foot from the lathered horse.

Mr. Whitney and I looked at each other for a pregnant moment without speaking. My breath came raggedly when it finally returned.

"You might have trampled me!"

"I didn't mean to frighten you," he said, jumping off his mount. He stood tall and lean before me, his white shirt a stark contrast to his darkened skin.

Feeling so disconcerted, I made no reply.

"Mourning becomes you," he said simply as he held the reins with the casual ease of a practiced horseman.

I flushed at the implication, knowing the color of my dress was bold and the stays on my corset were pulled in tighter than usual.

Though my cheeks burned, I held his gaze steadily and answered, "I haven't had time to unpack my things yet. My trunk was only just brought to me, as well as Minnie's—" I checked myself, pressing my lips tightly so they wouldn't tremble.

He looked impassively at me, my hesitation speaking for

itself. "Miss Dallsworth, you seem to have stumbled on your words. If we are to do this thing, we must do it properly."

"What do you mean?" I asked nervously, hoping to fool him.

"You referred to Minnie's trunk. You must remember *you* are Minnie." His horse snorted and pranced forward. Mr. Whitney stroked his back gently.

"Yes, of course." I was trying to feign nonchalance, but my voice quivered.

He watched me closely, but there was no hint of his derisive smile. It seemed he really believed that the only reason I claimed to be Maggie was because I had suffered a sort of shock. But why had Minnie become engaged to a man *she didn't know*?

My next comment was out before I could think. "Who are you, anyway? Why in the world did you become betrothed to a woman you don't know?"

He had moved with his horse several feet up the road; his back was to me. When he turned round, his face was defiant, his voice precise.

"Miss Dallsworth, if you have become conscious-stricken at the last moment, that's not my fault. But one thing is certain: We both have a great deal to gain, and I think it's in your interest as well as mine to keep quiet about this in the future and play our roles as if we meant them. It would be in both our favor to try and act as if we are in love."

I stared painfully at the arrogant figure in front of me. Oddly, he was right. Whoever he thought I was, there was freedom for me if I pretended to be his fianceé. But what was in it for him . . . ?

"Suppose you're right. Suppose we play these roles. What if someone finds out—"

"Don't be a fool." His voice snapped with exasperation. "Who is going to discover us?" His anger died, but his tone frightened me with its coldness. ''I assume you've left all your affairs in good order? No estranged husbands or heartsick beaus to come sniffing around?''

The power of his words hit me like a fist, and I recoiled. ''Are you afraid my past may interfere with what you have to gain?''

He wiped his forehead with the back of his hand. ''I don't give a damn about your past! But you sound so unnaturally anxious about carrying through with this, it makes me wonder if you're hiding something!''

''Me!'' I gasped breathlessly.

He reached down in one effortless swoop and plucked a mean-looking stick from the dirt. He stiffened, planted his legs apart and watched me with mild curiosity.

''Well. Are you?''

''Am I what?''

''Hiding something.''

''Nothing more than you're hiding!'' I choked out. His face was so dark, the stick so menacing, I could only ask, ''Are you threatening me?''

Then he smiled. An easy come-what-may grin, and his masculine face softened.

He threw his stick down and reached for the reins. ''Forgive me. It wasn't a gesture of aggression toward you, I . . . I'm not used to being around women.''

''And you, sir, should not be around women! You're arrogant and rude—and rather mean, into the bargain!''

He didn't flinch. ''I agree.''

That came as a surprise. All my womanlike fury and resolve were shaken to flinders. I opened my mouth to speak, but nothing came out.

''I'm sorry for all this, really I am.'' He stood very still. ''I hope I wasn't glib when I told you how nice you looked today.''

I found my voice again. ''I don't recall that you actually said I looked nice.''

"Well you do," he said without irritation. "At any rate, we've set the course now, haven't we? It's too late to retract. If you're holding back on me, I suppose I'll find out sooner or later. Now you should go find a black dress and wear it. Y' know, the funeral is tomorrow."

He was pushing the mare's head from side to side, playfully. It was evident I had been dismissed; our meeting was over, and he seemed suddenly bored with all of it. But I decided not to let him off so easily.

"Mr. Whitney, what . . . is there to be a wedding, then? I mean, between us?"

He regarded me without emotion. His face was expressionless, like carved stone. "Miss Dallsworth, I think I'd better let you know just where you stand with me. I don't like the idea of this wedding any more than you do. I am pleased to see you're not at all what I expected, but that isn't the point. You'll do well to keep out of my way and stay clear of Agate Bay. Go to Duluth whenever it pleases you, but take the trap, it's too far to walk—and pretend devotion to me."

In the silence that followed this remark, I heard a leaf rustle as it fell to earth with a thin, glassy sound.

Then he said in a dry, abrupt tone, "Don't look at me so oddly. You're gaining a husband and wealth and status. Isn't that what most women want?"

"Yes, I suppose so," I sighed wearily. I pulled my muddied heels from the thick soil and, surveying the dirty hem of my skirt, turned and left him standing there in the lane.

"Oh, Miss Dallsworth," he called after I had taken a few steps. "If it will relieve your fears at all, there will be no consummation of the marriage. So you can rest assured."

Whether it was relief or amazement that crossed my face, I can't be sure, but when I turned to look at him, he watched me with prying interest. There was something unspeakably offensive in his tone, in the words he used, and when I noted his insolent stance, my ire rose again.

Mumbling a "yes, of course," I fled from his ruthless gaze, down the winding path away from him, wondering how I could possible manage this charade.

Chapter 4

"Madam. My heartfelt condolences!" The voice caused me to turn from my position at the window.

The morning that had been thick with the threat of rain finally gave way to a torrential downpour.

"Thank you," I managed and let the heavy drape fall into place.

The somber pastor had entered noiselessly and was appraising me carefully from behind his steel glasses and stern brow. I shifted uncomfortably and noticed, for the first time, that the depressing dirge on the organ had ended. I was the last mourner to meet with the pastor, and I dreaded the interview.

Minnie and an elderly lady from Minnesota were the only two from the wreck to be buried in Duluth, the rest having been sent back to New York for funerals there. When Mr. Whitney asked where I thought Minnie should be laid to final rest, I could only reply that Duluth was fine. After all, I rationalized, we had no relatives left back East.

"Perhaps you should be seated, Miss Dallsworth."

I pulled up my veil and sank into the red velvet chair. Several gas lamps burned low and sputtered noisily. The heavily adorned parlor was aglow with them, their faltering light casting green shadows on the walls, and on the hard, angular lines of the pastor's face.

''Let us pray silently,'' came the pastor's whispered voice.

I hung my head and felt nothing. Only a great disdain for ceremony. After several moments' silence, the garish, velvet drapes at the doorway were pulled open to reveal a slim, pale man.

''Pastor, please excuse me but the hearses are leaving, everyone is—''

Pastor Bradley shot him a loaded look. ''Yes, of course. Thank you.''

I rose, covering my face with the veil. I knew Minnie's burial would be especially difficult. ''Thank you, Pastor.''

The clergyman held my gloved hands tightly, communicating his morbid interest in me. How similar in manner he was to Mrs. Svenson! As if the tragedies of others chillingly made their lives worthwhile.

''I am here for you, for your comfort in this time of loss. You may visit any time you wish. Do not worry about your beloved cousin Maggie Mansfield. She is at rest.''

I raised my eyes sharply at the sound of my name. My face must have registered the prick of apprehension that stung me, for his next words were: ''Do not be afraid. You are safe, and Mr. Whitney is waiting for you. We'll have your carriage pulled round. . . .''

But I didn't hear his words. We were heading toward the front parlor of the funeral home, through the shadowy rooms, where guests were leaving. The silk cloth of my gown rustled as I moved, reminding me that I was wearing Minnie's gown, not my own. I didn't have an appropriate dress, so I had had no choice.

''Are you all right?'' Mr. Whitney's voice was low and respectful.

''Yes, yes, I'll be fine,'' I agreed forlornly as I approached him.

I scrutinized the man before me. He wore a dark suit of fine cloth with silk-faced lapels and held his top hat. Though his mourning attire suited his lean body perfectly, there was something preposterous about it. He exuded such a vital energy that formal clothes seemed a mockery.

His glance in return touched on my lace-trimmed black dress, my hair pulled neatly back under the stiff boater with my veil, and he reached for my arm.

"Yes, she is doing quite well," the pastor said, placing a lavender-gloved hand on the small of my back.

Mr. Whitney gave him a look that bordered on contempt, and the pastor glanced quickly away, delicately touching the white cravat at his neck. They shook hands hurriedly, and the pastor ushered us out onto the wooden porch to wait for our conveyance.

I was glad to be on our way to the final destination. After a morning spent in the presence of grief—one old lady sobbed continually into her handkerchief—the cold, wet air felt intoxicating.

Mr. Whitney and I were silent as I clung to him going down the slippery steps, rain soaking us to the skin. At the bottom of the stairs there was a muddy gap between the wooden walkway and the carriage's bottom step. I faltered only a moment before I felt his strong arms grasp me easily and lift me gently into the buggy.

How ridiculous that my heart should skip a beat! I thought crazily as I slid into the soft leathery seat. His annoyingly cool presence, his distant appraisal of me, his fathomless eyes that reflected the color of the gray sky, all made me wary. And yet . . . my pulse seemed to quicken when he came close.

"Driver!" Mr. Whitney tapped his cane against the window and we jogged forward. I stared straight ahead, my beaded pursed clutched tightly in my hands.

"I've mentioned to a few of the townspeople that we will be married at the new St. Paul's Church as planned."

I glanced at him. He had removed his hat and his thick, wavy hair framed his manly head. He returned my look, his face a sculptured mask, his eyes unwavering.

"Yes, I supposed we must," I said tonelessly.

Suddenly his face lightened and he regarded me frankly, reflectively. "It can hardly be avoided. The wedding, I mean. If we're to continue with our scheme with any timeliness. After all, my railroad can't wait. The September deadline must be met, and there'll be no time then to bother with weddings and other such nonsense."

His words were plain and honest, yet they stung. Even in their simplicity they were edged with steel.

I swallowed nervously.

Scheme . . . railroad. Was this it, then? Had Minnie agreed to marry a man as part of some sort of business deal involving a railroad? Hadn't she mentioned that her fiancé was clearing a path up through a wilderness to haul out some mineral by train? What was it that she said he was digging . . . ? Gold, iron ore? My heart lurched at the thought of nearing the truth. Why not ask outright?

"I don't recall hearing too much about your railroad," I tossed out carelessly, waiting for a reproach from him. There was no reply.

I glanced up and saw that he was ignoring me. He looked very faraway as he watched the splatters of rain roll down the windows.

"No, I suppose you wouldn't," he said finally.

"Don't you think it's rather extraordinary that I don't know anything about your work?" I tested him and he knew it.

"Not really. It's rather what I expected, to be honest." He gave me an arrogant glance as our carriage thundered to a halt.

"Oh," I exhaled raggedly and turned from his gaze. I choked back the sob that suddenly welled within me.

The ability to say what I pleased seemed to liberate my carefully hidden emotions. My throat ached and my eyes burned as I struggled to fight back the threatening tears. Not since my marriage had I felt so bereft and alone—as, indeed, I was now. Minnie was the last of my relatives.

As Mr. Whitney helped me down from the carriage, I

wondered, dismally, if my pain came from Minnie's loss or from the dizzyingly unpredictable situation I was in.

There was no answer for that. Mr. Whitney sensed my dismay and gallantly offered his arm, which I accepted once more. His harshness had faded, and without so much as a word, I felt he understood me. And, strangely, also understood my loneliness. As we tramped through the muddy wilderness of the graveyard toward Minnie's plot, I was aware of the damp material of his coat close to my skin, the clean odor of soap and talc.

A narrow path wound through flowering underbrush and thick, squat bushes. We crested a hill where there was a strip of lonely burial ground. The rain fell in gusting sheets and the wind howled miserably. In a momentary silence, I heard the dull beating of the surf below us. A dreary sound at a dreary hour.

Overhead, lost in the blanket of cloud cover, a crow called. The weird, primitive sound died as I watched the casket being lowered into the earth. I glanced up, away from the horrifying scene, and noticed the bleak silhouette of the church and its line of picket fence.

When I looked back, a huge, brawny man, completely covered in oilskin, heaved his shovel into the ground. He lifted the first scoop of black dirt and poured it into the grave.

Too cold to bear the weather any longer, we trudged away, passing the marble tombstone that was ready to be put in place. It was inscribed:

AT REST
MAGDELA MANSFIELD
BORN MAY 1861, DIED JUNE 1884

I shuddered miserably.

That night a terrible darkness fell. There was too much pain for me to sit idly and read, so I passed the evening hours by sorting through the still-packed clothes and personal items that belonged to Minnie and myself.

Having calculated that no one knew what belonged to whom, I combined our worldly possessions and came up with a surprisingly tasteful assortment of gowns and accessories. Using my empty portmanteau, I filled it with dresses and suits that I'd be most unlikely to wear. These would be put into storage, I assumed, and labeled the "deceased woman's wardrobe."

At the end of my evening's efforts, I was disappointed not to have found so much as a clue to Minnie's dubious relationship to Mr. Whitney. There was nothing. Not a passionate love letter, a locket with a smiling photograph, not even a dried flower in a book . . .

Disappointed, I collected all the pieces of rich materials purchased for Minnie's dresses. The fabric was heavy, but I managed to pile it together on an armchair in my dressing room. Next I carried my wicker basket of sewing implements and my mannequin into the little room. I set the dummy up in the center of the room and laid out my sewing things—pins, needles, thread and so on. There! I smiled. I had at least created a dressmaker room for myself.

Lighting the small alabaster urns on the wall, I delighted in what a good area I had for work. It was small, but I could lay my materials out on the long dressing table, and the light was good. A piece of glimmering white caught my eye as I turned to go. The wedding gown, I mused ironically.

Spurred by my successful attempt at creating a workspace, I took on another challenge. My rooms had been deep in gloom all night, partly because there was no fire. I went to the grate. Rose had carefully laid the kindling for me, and when I lit it, the flames caught at once. The fire roared up and soothed me with its gentle hissing. With the fire crackling cheerfully, I set about adding some personal touches to my chambers.

On the secretary I placed a few tokens from home that I treasured dearly. I carefully arranged the Meissen gold-and-blue tea set from Mother on the marble-topped table at the room's center, caressing the fine smooth edges, the underglaze of powder blue. I remembered Mother's gentle hands and her laughing voice as she poured tea for the great ladies of the theater. She had possessed a unique talent as a dressmistress, and I hoped I had inherited it.

Gently I blew dust off the stack of books Father had given me. Among them were several contemporary writers of great merit and, of course, the book Father treasured the most—*Ivanhoe*. His name, in fact, was synonymous with Ivanhoe, for he had played the role so many times he had become famous. I lined the books along one of the deep windowsills and sighed happily. No room could remain dreary with books.

I had finished placing other odds and ends about the room when a pang of melancholy struck me. The lovely reminders of my childhood were warming, yet they suggested a life that was gone. To dispel my somber mood, I decided to try the plate of dinner Rose had brought only an hour ago.

The cold leg of chicken, slab of cheese, butter and twist of crusty bread tasted exceedingly good. I sipped the surprisingly delicate red wine and felt a warm contentment creep over me.

I leaned back on the tufted chaise lounge and closed my eyes. The hot flames of fire warmed me, causing thoughts of my dreadful day to melt away.

I fell to dreaming. I dreamt of a day five years ago when Clyde and I held the first ball in our New York town house. The bushels of roses, bottles of champagne, the orchestra, the guest list with formidable names, all came alive for me again.

Abruptly the dream changed. The strains of music ceased, the guests disappeared and the house was empty. Like a spirit possessed with supernatural powers, I soared up to the front door and read a notice attached there. RENT NOT PAID. TENANTS EVICTED.

I passed through the wood, like a puff of smoke, and

entered the still house. Only a few remnants of our lives remained, and they lay scattered, like debris, upon the tile floor. A scrap of writing paper, a broken lambrequin from a window, an old shoelace.

The soulless, desolate house was cold and so very empty. And in my dream, as in real life, the gas had been turned off, the servants long ago dismissed.

"Madam . . . ? Miss Dallsworth?"

I sat up, startled. There was a rapping at my door. Without a moment to think, I called, "Come in."

Rose walked in quietly. She glanced around the room before her anxious eyes lit on me. I noticed that she wore no cap. Her graying hair was puffed and curled in an attempt to make it look thicker than it was. She wore a plain skirt and a blouse covered with blue satin bows, and despite her age she looked youthful and pretty.

I moved to get up, a piece of unruly hair falling over my forehead. It took me a moment to realize that I had fallen asleep, and I blushed at being caught so off-guard.

"Ye must be very tired," she said gently.

"Oh, yes. The day has been so long . . . please, what time do you have? There doesn't seem to be a clock in my room."

She peered closer, her green eyes questioning me. "Why, m'lady. Have ye forgotten? Y'er wearin' a gold watch pin."

Hastily I looked down. The gold watch of Minnie's! I had carefully pinned it to my bodice and had forgotten it was there.

"Oh, oh. How silly of me," I stammered out, blood rushing to my temples. "Yes, well. Ten o'clock is not so late, is it?"

Her eyebrows raised slightly as she answered, "No, not so late."

She waited a moment before she spoke again, and I wondered with a deepening dread if I seemed unusually odd to her.

"Master Whitney would like to see you at once in the

parlor if . . . y'er properly awake. But I could tell him y'er not awa—''

"No. Don't do that. Tell him I'll see him. Just give me a moment to . . . pull myself together.''

She smiled rather uncertainly and left. Why I felt such a compulsion to hurry down to Mr. Whitney immediately, I didn't know. Damn the man! I cursed to myself. He held a power over me that appeared to be diabolical.

I stood at the cheval mirror and removed the plait in my hair, twisting it instead into a knot. I stopped short and looked at myself. It was obvious that I was excited. My cheeks were flushed to an unnatural brightness and my eyes snapped with animation.

He can't do this to me, that's all! I'm a sensible woman who must appear to have a no-nonsense manner. I must not be the trembling violet, the lovelorn woman afraid of her man, as I once was. Those dark days are over.

What am I saying? I frowned. Mr. Whitney is *not* my man! I am only playing a role!

Hurridly I brushed out the wrinkles in my mourning dress and noticed that the gleam in my eyes was softening; my cheeks were returning to their normal color.

Having regained my dignity, I left my rooms and ventured down the hall. Behind a closed door I heard a man's laughter, and I paused. Perhaps there were other occupants in this desolate place after all.

I moved quietly down the stairs and, at the bottom, I turned to my left. I had noticed this room before and could find it easily.

The door was open wide, as the parlor was available to guests. My footfall on the leaf-patterned carpet was silent, so Mr. Whitney didn't hear me enter. He sat in the center of the room at an unadorned Penbroke writing table. An oil lamp burned brightly next to him, but the rest of the gold-and-red room was deep in gloom. I studied him a moment as he sat in the halo of light, writing intently. He wore a pair of spectacles and his brows were creased in concentration.

I was about to knock, but he looked up abruptly before I could move. Our eyes held a moment before his unsmiling, rapier glance passed over me in a flicker of an instant. I was glad for the shadows because I flushed deeply.

He stood up, hastily folding the sheet of paper he had been so busily working on, sticking it in his vest pocket. "Please, come in. I know it's late, but I forgot to give you something that I think you'll want to have."

"Yes, thank you," I replied, trying to control my thumping heart.

I accepted the chair he offered me and glanced around. A low fire burned in the tile fireplace, but it leant little illumination to the rest of the room. Several jet globes burned high on the wall, but the gasolier overhead was unlit. Red tones dominated the room, from the few small groupings of velvet chairs to the deep color in the mahogany wood. It was a distinctively masculine room; there was a lingering scent of tobacco and oil.

He regarded me a moment before he picked up a small package wrapped in brown paper from the desk. He walked close and handed it to me.

"This is for you."

I hoped my face didn't betray the alarm I felt. Who was sending this package, and why? With a hapless smile I accepted the gift, noticing that a note was attached. There was a shock for me when my eyes lit on the postmark from New York!

I kept my lashes lowered to hide the fear in my eyes. I tore open the sealed envelope. The brief missive was written in small, almost tortured letters, and it read:

> My dearest,
>
> This will come to you once you've arrived safely, I hope. You are in Charles's care now, and may he be agreeable to you! Ha! If you need money, remember to

ask Charles. He'll take care of you. Don't disappoint him. We need him for now. Write soon and let me know how you're faring. And is your cousin making that promised gown for the wedding?

There was no signature, no initial even. A shiver of foreboding brought me to the edge of my chair. There was a conspiratorial ring to the letter, and it frightened me. Who was this letter from, and what was I expected to say?

I glanced up. Mr. Whitney sat on the corner of the small desk, with one leg swinging, his cool gray eyes fixed on me. His fine form was lit by the pool of lamplight on the table. My glance touched upon his tossled dark hair, his vest hanging casually open, his collarless shirt without a tie, his spectacles dangling on the end of a chain.

"What does he say?"

"Nothing . . . at all. Only . . . only that he misses me." My voice was surprisingly low and even.

"Oh. I only thought he'd mention when he planned to visit you."

I felt my face pale and struggled for an answer. "No . . . there was no mention of a visit."

"I'm sorry. It's been a long day. The funeral was worse for you than I imagined." A gleam of compassion lit his eyes. "Why don't you open his gift, then I'll take you back to your rooms."

"Yes, it's been a long day," I murmured raggedly. Trying to still my trembling hands, I opened the mysterious parcel.

Inside the velvet box was an exquisite pair of diamond-and-pearl pendant earrings with a matching seed pearl and diamond locket. I lifted them out. The diamonds caught the firelight and sparkled with a thousand colors.

"The set is lovely," I said hollowly. If I only had some idea how to behave, knew who this valuable gift was from. . . .

"It's about time—" Mr. Whitney's voice was near. He

had risen from the desk and stood admiring the jewelry. "—that he sent you something so worthy of you."

I marshaled my whirling thoughts and tried to act nonchalant, as Minnie would if presented with such a gift. "Yes, this gift has been late in coming."

I was aware of his eyes on me, brooding, suspicious. After an unhappy pause, I stood, eager to be away from his scrutiny.

He took the clue and offered his arm. "Can I walk you upstairs, then?"

"That would be fine," I agreed hastily.

I entwined my arm with his and once more that day felt his raw strength underneath the shirt's fine cloth. The foyer was empty, as it always seemed to be, and boards creaked under our feet as we moved up the twisting stairs, down the shadowy corridor. There was no conversation, and an uneasy tension rose like a cloud between us.

At my own room, he gave me a long look, close and enigmatic.

"Good night, then, and I hope you're feeling stronger tomorrow."

I hesitated. "Good night, Mr. Whitney."

He leaned impatiently against the wall. "You're still determined . . . look, if we're going to play this game with any authenticity, you can hardly call me 'Mr. Whitney.'"

"Perhaps," I answered huskily, "you're right. From now on, I'll call you Charles and you can call me Minnie."

"Good. Sometimes I wonder how the hell we got involved like this, but well," his voice was full of exasperation, "here we are." His eyes held mine a moment, then he leaned over suddenly and kissed my hand. "Minnie," he said softly, then turned and walked away.

I opened the door, thinking it unnecessary to lock it with the latchkey Mrs. Svenson had given me and wondered, with horror, how dangerous Charles might, in fact, be. How disquieting that I would gravitate toward such a man, a man obviously bent on achieving a selfish goal. At any cost.

What deal had been struck between Minnie and this invisible third party, and why? Perhaps it was this faceless, nameless person that I should turn to. Perhaps I should answer his letter. . . .

As I quickly undressed and lowered the cock on my lamp, I knew that, indeed, Charles wasn't the only one with a secret. How could I mistrust him? doubt his motives? when I, in fact, had a secret of my own. After all, I was a divorced woman—running from her half-mad husband.

Chapter 5

The next morning I was up early. I pulled the drapes open to find a luminous sun shining. The wide sky, the touch of dewy air upon my face and gleam of sunlight glinting off the water's surface made me eager to leave my rooms.

I dressed in a serviceable gown of off-black with balloon sleeves, pulled my hair back into a rolled knot with matching onyx combs and went downstairs in search of breakfast. There was no telling what was expected of me, but I knew what Minnie would do: She would become mistress of the manor. Although no one at the inn had even met the real Minnie, it helped me to imagine her bold response to the situation I found myself in.

She would eat when she was hungry, give orders to the service staff and make glib comments within hearing of the guests about how unrefined the inn really was. And she would have been right about the inn's plainness.

Yet the thick white walls and soaring ceilings were not created as a monument, they were made for simple shelter. There was an honesty about the structure; there were no rooms stuffed with gaudy, ornamental furnishings. The architecture of the inn was as frank and unadorned as the man who owned it.

I swept the thought out of my mind as I moved along the narrow corridor, twin alabaster globes lending a soft light to the hallway. When I reached the mahogany doorway of the dining room, I was surprised to find the room filled with noisy laughter and conversation. There must have been at least a dozen men seated at the linen-covered tables arranged about the airy room.

Muted sunlight filtered through the filmy white curtains at the enormous windows. The room radiated a warmth that seemed to emanate from the foiled cream walls and burnished copper carpets.

I paused to find a table, noticing how particularly unkempt the boisterous men were. Their gray suits seemed frayed and badly in need of mending. In an instant I concluded what made this group different. They were broad-faced, big-boned giants with pale skin and blond hair. I imagined them as lumberjacks or Vikings sailing on grim-prowed ships.

How different their coarse manners were compared to Charles's raw, yet civilized, vitality! I blushed deeply at my unutterable thoughts and turned away from the unguarded stares aimed at my direction.

"Is there not a table to your liking, Madam Dallsworth?" I whirled around at the sound of the name.

Before me stood a tall, lanky gentleman with matted yellow hair and a greased handlebar mustache. He was dressed in the same moss green the bellboy had worn yesterday. I assumed he was the *maitre d'hotel.*

"Oh, I was only looking . . . I didn't expect people." My words were out before I could catch them. How odd he must think I am! I thought stupidly as he led me to a window table.

"It's a busy time for Mr. Whitney. As you know, the railroad will be finished soon and all these men . . . well, we have a new engineer with us today, several new foremen for the mines and even Captain Flynn from the *Ella G. Stone.* Guess Mr. Whitney needs as many hands as possible." He smiled tentatively.

"Yes, I suppose you're right," I replied vaguely. He seated me, bowing stiffly, but made no move to go.

"Is the *Ella G. Stone* a boat?" I asked foolishly.

"Oh, yes, madam, a tugboat. Why I see it 'round here all the time. It's always leavin' from the makeshift dock here on the inn's land—in order to carry men to the worksite up north."

I smiled ignorantly.

"Last year Contractor Whitney employed near to six hundred men for work on the railroad. This year, since the deadline draws near, he's got darn close to fourteen thousand! Workin' round the clock, too! He's a hard drivin' man, I hear, but fair, Madam Dallsworth!"

"Yes, he is, isn't he?" I commented nervously.

I felt him survey me with reproachful eyes. As if he knew something was peculiar. Damn! There must be a way to rid myself of the guilt, that lingering sense of self. After all no one here had met Minnie before. This deception could be easy if it weren't for my anxiety.

"The railroad . . ." I tried to remember the name of the town Charles had bade me stay away from. Yes, Agate Shore! that was it. ". . . is it being built in the town of Agate Shore?"

The man tossed me a blank look before replying. "Er, if you mean Agate Bay, madam, that's the place."

"Oh, of course!" I laughed rather too shrilly. "How could I forget such an easy name?" I sipped nervously from my water goblet.

Determined to end the awkward conversation, I ordered fresh peaches with cream and coffee. I was glad to see him nod silently and leave.

I tried to act content with eating alone. The coffee was strong and rich, and the peaches melted in my mouth, but all the while I was nervously aware of the guests' undisguised curiosity. Finally I rose to leave and made one last infuriating blunder. If the waiter thought I was odd at the beginning of breakfast, he surely thought me mad at the end.

Unsure of how money was to be handled—was I a guest or, in fact, a resident?—I asked, embarrassingly, for the check. He froze in a half bow and spoke in low tones.

"Madam, you are not to pay for anything. I thought Mr. Whitney had made that plain to you befor—"

"Oh yes! Of course! I should have remembered . . . it was stupid of me to forget something so important. My husband, uh, fiancé, told me to do anything I please," I stammered uneasily and, smiling feebly, vanished from the room posthaste.

I made my way hurridly back through the shadowy hall, toward the foyer. When I emerged into the entranceway there was a buzz of activity. Several black bags lay scattered upon the carpeted floor. Two gaunt-faced gentlemen stood talking to a nodding porter, while the frail bellboy hoisted a huge valise onto his shoulders.

The front door stood open. A blade of brilliant blue contrasted with the dark interior, and I moved quickly toward it.

"Madam, would you like a cab?" I stopped and turned back to the inquiring porter. I had been unable to sneak out unnoticed.

"A cab?" I repeated lamely.

"To go shopping, or perhaps to sightsee?"

I hadn't thought of either, but why not visit Duluth again? I had seen only a smear of dirty buildings through rain-spattered windows yesterday. Suddenly the thought of visiting the little town piqued my interest, and I told him that, yes, I would need a conveyance.

His hand was on the bell immediately, and shortly a sturdy landau pulled up for me. I climbed in as soon as the stairs were let down, and we moved off down the windy road. We traveled south, past spindly birch and aspen trees, along a rutted road thick with mud. We approached the bustling city by way of Superior Street.

I was let off at the northern end of town and decided to

take my chances on the shops located there. The day sped by in windowshopping and trying to find bargains. Perhaps a length of lace for a fischu or satin ribbons for trim. I always delighted in handling, touching, sorting through fabric, even though there was nothing I urgently needed.

It was late when I finally purchased a yard of battenberk lace and emerged onto the street again. The trim row of crackerbox storefronts was etched in a dull white against the salty sky. The earlier crystalline air of the lakeside town was fading and clouds moved in from the west. A warm, gusty wind began to blow, and it smelled like rain again.

Clutching my parcel to me, I managed to cross a wooden plank over the mired street to get to the Grant Hotel, where an empty cab waited.

"Hi, cabbie!" I called, approaching the fly. "Are you for hire?" As I spoke, I noticed a bundle of luggage stacked under the box.

"Yer'll have to inquire inside, miss. I been spoken for," came the bored response.

The lobby was deep in gloom, and it took a moment before my eyes focused on the hum and clamour around me. It was instantly apparent that newly arrived guests were checking in.

Before I could ask for a cab, a woman swathed in black seemed to rise, like a shadow, from a dark corner. She placed a lace-covered hand on a porter's arm, forcing him to turn his look upon her. I was so close to them it was impossible not to hear her question, spoken in broken English with a French accent. I tried to move unobtrusively around the pile of luggage, but her words riveted me, and I was forced to stop and listen.

"*Monsieur,* will you kindly direct me to the Duluth and Iron Range Railroad? You know the offices of Charles Whitney? I have traveled a great distance to see him."

I drew in a breath and heard the porter reply nonchalantly, "Oh yes, his offices are jus' round the corner there, on Lake and Superior Street. Can' miss 'em."

"*Merci beaucoup, monsieur.*" Her hands were as fluid as water as she dropped a coin in his palm and rustled past me, a scent of lilac lingering in the air.

A prickly sense of self-doubt welled up inside me. Jealousy? That was too strong a word. But my heart hammered crazily in my head and my knees were weak. I should have known, should have suspected. A man like Charles—alone in this wilderness?

Groping for the porter's sleeve, I asked frantically, "Please, sir, could you tell me, did a train just arrive?"

He hardly lifted a brow as he savagely pulled out a portmanteau stuck on the bottom of the pile. "Yes, ma'am. Not half an hour ago. The Great Northern . . . just down the block on Lakeshore if yer' collectin' someone."

"No, I wasn't waiting for anyone, I just wondered"—The man stood, his face beaded with sweat—"where it was coming from?"

"St. Paul, ma'am, where all trains connect that's comin' from the East." With a grunt he regarded me blankly before moving away with his burden.

From the East. Yes! She had to be. A floating, limpid beauty who had traveled all this way . . .

Without bothering to ask for a cab, I stepped outside again. I was just in time to witness the driver of the waiting hack close the door and pull up the steps. I caught a glimpse of the woman's veiled face framed by the window before the cab sped away.

I stood a moment, lost in thought, when a gust of wind lifted the silk of my skirts. The wind was rising again.

"Hello! Waiting for a cab?" A toothless driver leered down at me from another hack that had just pulled up.

My intense anxiety over the mysterious woman's appearance made me fail to appreciate the conveyance. Without skipping a beat I climbed into the cab and gave the address "Witch Tree Inn," as we started forward.

We trotted past Lake Street, and I looked out the window at the stone building on the corner. I caught the words

DULUTH AND IRON RANGE RAILROAD on a black sign before glancing at the men in the street. They were rolling wooden barrels down to the edge of the sidewalk and straining hard as if the containers were heavy.

There was little to distinguish him by his dress, but I recognized Charles immediately because he seemed quicker and more agile in his movements than the others. His coat hung carelessly open; he was hatless; his face worked in a grimace. The veiled lady had been looking for him. Had she found him already? Why wasn't she with him now? Perhaps they would wait until the blue hour of evening to embrace. . . .

I felt the hot blood rush to my cheeks and turned away hastily.

I saw nothing of Charles that evening or for the week that followed. It didn't surprise me, though. There was a great flurry of activity at the inn; men were coming and going, talking in deliberate voices of business concerns, feasting and drinking. It seemed that some turning point in the railroad's construction had been reached, and Charles was immersed in negotiations.

I had little time to notice all the mayhem since I was caught in my own sticky, entrapping web. Mrs. Svenson was full of the thrill of planning the wedding—my wedding.

For, as Charles had bitterly informed me earlier, the wedding ceremony would be on time—despite the funeral. He had made it quite clear that he could not afford to leave his work on the railroad any other day.

The wedding was to be quite small and simple. Pastor Bradley would recite the vows—of course!—and only a handful of people would attend.

I was inextricably pulled into Mrs. Svenson's world of tedious details, mindless tasks and boring protocol. It was obvious that Mrs. Svenson had no daughters and this was her only chance at a mother's glory hour.

Deciding that none of this mattered to me anyway—and

wasn't it best to keep busy to avoid thinking about Charles?—I let her have her way. When she suggested that my tussah silk gown, webbed with fine silver thread, was too plain, I decided that a fancier veil was in store. It was sheer lunacy to follow Mrs. Svenson's tasteless advice on clothes, but I wanted to keep busy. I sketched several versions of my new veil before making a pattern. Then I cut out a lovely length of French lace, purchased by Minnie in New York, and trimmed it with satin ribbon. Once this was achieved, I started the endless process of covering the material with tiny seed pearls.

Thus, suspended in my globe of work, the week before the wedding passed quickly. All the while I kept trying to ignore disturbing imaginings of that dark mystery woman with Charles. If Minnie had planned to marry Charles for financial gain, how could I seem jealous? I must keep a level, logical head. How could I so foolishly allow Charles to make me quake?

One soft evening just before the wedding, as a golden dusk lent ruby light to my room, Rose entered with her usual tray of dinner. I stood to greet her, the spread of lace I had been working on billowing to the floor. I immediately engaged her in conversation, for I could endure the isolation of my work no longer.

"Please, won't you take coffee with me?" I went to the small round table where she set the tray and fell exhausted into one of the chairs.

"Thank ye, m'lady. But can' stay long, Mrs. Svenson's got flowers waitin' for me to arrange in the kitchen." Yet she sat anyway, in the chair across from me.

I laughed suddenly. "I've no doubt! Marrying and burying is the stuff of life to her."

Her tired face came alight. "Perhaps y'er right! I wish Mr. Whitney'd never hired her. Things was so much better before." She looked down.

"Before?" I waited. She extended a oxford-clad foot and stared at it.

"Before Mr. Whitney bought the inn, m'lady."

"What was the inn like then?"

"It was elegant. I mean for these parts, anyhow. There was political meetins held in the big dinin' room downstairs, and always much hustle and bustle of carriages pullin' up and leavin'. He's, I mean the master, Mr. Whitney, changed thins', taken out lots of furniture, stored stuff in the old lighthouse keeper's cottage next door."

I said quickly, "I didn't know there was a lighthouse next door. Is it still in use?"

"Oh no, m'lady," she paused and sipped her coffee, "ain't been fer some time. Guess Mr. Whitney sort of inherited it when he bought Witch Tree Inn. Don' know what else he's got stored there, but—"

She stood, suddenly distracted, her face shining with delight. "M'lady! Yer gown is so beautiful! See how it shimmers in the light. Oh, won't you be lovely!"

I joined her at the bedside, where the gossamer gown lay, smiling at her enthusiasm. "I'm glad you like it. See . . . my new veil is almost finished and—" I picked up the fluff of lace on the floor and held up the delicate material. It shimmered in the glowing half light. "—I think it will go well with my dress."

She clasped her hands happily, her cheeks reddening. "Oh, m'lady!"

An inspiration came to me. "Rose, when the wedding is over I'll have plenty of time to myself. Would you like me to make you a dress? I'd love doing that for you. It would make me so happy."

"Oh, m'lady, Madam Dallsworth! I didn't dare ask, but if you could . . . oh, if you could . . . my brother's gettin' married the end of summer, and I would sure love a new dress."

I was as excited as she was. "Then it's a deal. We'll go to town together, buy the material, and I can start as soon as I'm able."

Her excitement was almost childlike, and she thanked me

repeatedly while exclaiming over my gown. Touching the fine material gently as if it were a religious relic, she said, "Mr. Whitney will be so pleased!"

The comment sent my heart to fluttering, although I knew I shouldn't care if my appearance would please him. I was marrying him for practical reasons. And certainly not for love!

Trying to act as though I were unmoved, I said casually, "You know, Rose, he's been an enigma to me all the time I've known him." I was fingering a seed pearl. "He's lived here alone, for . . . how long has it been now? I honestly can't remember." I laughed hoarsely.

"He's only been here about two years now, that I recall. Least he was here when I was hired, but I know that he come jus' before me."

I glanced away from her inquiring look. "Yes," I said suddenly. "It seems so long. When you're in love, y'know, separation can be endless." I bit my lip. Some deep anxiety caused my next question to slip out before I could check it.

"Rose," I said in a conspiratorial whisper, "several days ago a woman dressed in black arrived in Duluth to meet Charles. Now I'm not insinuating anything"—I placed my palm dramatically over my chest and tried to feign a laugh—"I only wondered if . . . if she was staying here or if you may have seen Charles with her. I don't even know what she looks like; she wore a veil the day I saw her."

"Yes, jus' several days ago I seen a tall, willowly lady wearin' a veil! I wouldna' noticed her except that I figured she was in mournin'. But I niver seen Mr. Whitney with her." She glanced away from me in embarrassment, the direct question obviously causing her discomfort.

My obstinate determination to solve the riddle of the woman's appearance had exhausted my good manners, and I apologized. "I'm sorry, Rose. I'm acting as foolish as a schoolgirl! It's only that I didn't have a chance to know Charles well before accepting his hand in marriage. . . ."

Her eyebrows raised thoughtfully. We stared silently at

each other for a whirling moment. "Does anybody know who they's marryin'?" A thin smile touched her mouth.

Rose left me then, making her apologies and saying that Mrs. Svenson would be in a fiddle-faddle if she didn't appear to do the flowers soon. Her departure left me in a state of depression. Had I been too eager, asked too much? I was careening dangerously toward some dark secret, and I wasn't sure if I wanted to discover it.

Shrugging off my misgivings, I resolved then and there to put my apprehensions aside and enjoy the wedding.

A bouquet bursting with honeysuckle, tiny pink roses and gardenias, laced with baby's breath and heather, and tied round in satin ribbon lay ready upon my chaise lounge. The blooms filled the room with their intoxicating scent, and a thrill of excitement touched me.

It was my first twinge of emotion. Because I was like a spectator at a play, I hadn't felt involved. This day had been planned for another woman, the gown designed for someone else. Why, then, was I here now? All the preparations for the other woman's wedding had come neatly together, and I watched, distantly, as an onlooker might.

A little before noon, Rose helped me dress. There were numerous hooks and eyes to be fastened, tapes to be tied. My silk dress slid on smoothly over my well-boned corset and sleek-fitted petticoats. The wedding gown was simple and graceful, with a soft train flowing out the back. My hair was plaited and tied with the same satin ribbon that trimmed my veil. I slipped into silk-covered shoes and pulled on my kid gloves.

Taking my cue from Rose's inhalation of breath, I moved to the full-length mirror. My eyes sparkled, and I smiled a little too gaily as I regarded my reflection.

"I feel like a bride," I said, my voice quivering.

"You *are* a bride, m'lady! And what a lovely one ye are, too!"

"'This is the night that either makes me or fordoes me quite,'" I recited hollowly.

"M'lady, there is not much time. Mr. Whitney will be waiting at the chur— Oh fiddle! I almost forgot to give yer this." She pulled a crumpled sealed envelope from the front of her apron and gave it to me.

She rushed away, calling, "I have to dress, m'lady, or I'll be sure to miss the wedding meself!"

It was too much to hope that the letter was sent by Charles. He'd been only a ghostly presence these last days. But I yearned for a sign from him, for some form of communication . . .

The envelope was stamped from New York. My hands shook as I tore it open.

My darling,

What has happened? I would have thought you'd written me by now. Has Charles been treating you badly or something? What's the trouble? I'm in no mood to deal with Charles's cut-throat machinations. If there is trouble with him, tell me. There's no telling what he'd do to get his way!

I stared incredulously at the mysterious message. A sense of terrible doom choked me, and I threw the offending letter into the cold grate, lighting it with a taper. A red tongue of flame flared up and licked it, burning the foolscap immediately.

I was ready to barter this role, my fascination for Charles, if I could only have my old life back. So what that I lived in fear of Clyde? Was living like this any better? How could I keep deceiving the world when, in fact, it was deceiving me?

In a last, almost unthinking, gesture, I put on the pendent earrings and fastened the matching diamond locket around my neck. A ray of light caught a diamond and it shone like fire.

"Madam! Are you ready?" There came a pounding on my door.

"Miss Dallsworth?!" Mrs. Svenson's voice was edged with hysteria. Her day, her accomplishment. What was any of this to me, except possible trickery and peril?

"Yes! I'm coming. You'll have to help me with my veil." I darted out the door so fast I was thrust into the lacey bosom of the reigning matriarch.

She dripped with bows and lilac organza frills. "Ohhh! You are a dream, my child. Come we *must* hurry! And, oh, here, let me properly attach your headpiece, so, and your train must be held up to avoid the muddy streets . . ." Her voice trailed me down the surprisingly vacated stairs, along the ghostly corridor and into the revealing sunlight to the waiting carriage.

The landau bumped along the rutted road for several miles before stopping in front of a crude wood-frame church at the edge of town. There was a small gathering of plump ladies garbed in their Sunday clothes waiting at the steps. I glanced at Mrs. Svenson. No doubt they were her friends.

Slowly, as if my movements were not my own but belonged to a bride in a fairy tale, I descended the carriage and entered the dimness of the church's interior. My veil was lowered over my face, my train was laid flat and chords from the pipe organ filled the air.

The oak doors that separated me from the chapel were opened, and I moved, in my swirl of white, toward the towering, dangerous man standing before me.

Chapter
6

His fathomless gray eyes seemed to drink me up, and I returned his stare. As I took my place next to him, I heard his deep, low exhalation.

"You're lovely!" His words were spoken so softly they were meant only for me.

I was so foolishly overcome by emotion that I looked down and made a feeble attempt to calm my frightening thoughts. I was falling in love with this man! It was true that he was thrilling to behold, that his masculine appeal transcended his dashing black morning jacket with crisp shirt and tie, but he couldn't be trusted and was most likely mean-spirited and a threat to my life.

The bitter morsel of truth was hard to swallow. I had married a man once before because of a passionate attraction. A man who was desperately unhappy because his career was doomed and he was penniless. Naively thinking that love could mend all wounds, I tried to make him happy. But his failure to make money made him spiteful . . . and cruel.

Wasn't it always about money, then? I glanced quickly at Charles's aquiline profile. What was under his tightly controlled, simmering surface? Who did he think he was marrying, and how much money had he to gain? Oh,

Minnie, Minnie, what a sinister entanglement I've gotten myself into!

Pastor Bradley's service was mercifully short, but his low voice rang with religious fervor and bravado. My voice trembled as we spoke our vows, and I felt the intensity of the few guests as they strained forward on their benches to hear.

"With this ring I thee wed," came Charles's voice. When he looked at me his face was set, austere, and his eyes were dark. In a fleeting moment I thought perhaps he was controlling some attraction he felt toward me. . . .

Without a gesture of tenderness, but without scorn, either, he placed a simple gold circle on my finger. It was sprinkled with tiny diamonds and complemented the larger, gaudier engagement ring.

There was to be no ring for Charles. Of course! I thought suspiciously. This was not a real marriage for him, there were other women . . .

"May all that is noble and lovely and true abide with you forever. You may kiss the bride."

My heart stopped. I had forgotten this detail of the ceremony! With practiced ease, he lifted the veil from my face and bent his head to me. In a roaring moment, I felt his hand on my back, inhaled the clean scent of talc, felt his mustache brush my mouth . . .

His kiss was firm and hard, without desire, his arm on my back steady, but as he released me I caught a burning glint in his eyes. He turned away a little too rapidly.

Charles tucked my arm through his, and to the strains of the organ, we marched down the aisle. A rain of rice fell on us as we stepped out the door into the brilliant sunlight. Garlands of pale pink and white peonies decorated the waiting landau.

Without a word between us we climbed into our conveyance, and to the sound of women's laughter and applause, we drove away. Down the lane, past low hills of smooth boulders, mounds of upturned dirt from road crews, scrubby bushes and pinpricks of pastel wildflowers, we sped. The sparrows and gulls and a dozen odd assortments of birds flew about, their thin songs echoing ecstatically through the balmy air. We rounded a curve, and the glassy surface of the lake came into view, that expanse of sapphire that seemed to stretch to the end of the earth.

I glanced at his profile, realizing that neither of us had spoken for some time. Now that we were alone there was little to say.

"What happens now?" the comfort of saying something, anything, to break our silence prompted my query.

He gazed at me, his eyes hooded, guarded. "I thought he would have told you."

I couldn't hide my skepticism. "Well, he didn't, and I would like to know what my role is to be now." My honesty surprised me. But it didn't seem to betray me, for he said rather harshly, "Damn the man! What does he expect of me?"

I suddenly glanced away, afraid he'd catch my puzzled look.

"I see you've worn them," he shot out suddenly.

"What?"

"The earrings and locket he gave you." His tone was unnaturally severe, as if he were accusing me of something.

"Oh," I said with surprise. "Yes, I thought they went rather well with my gown."

"Yes, I suppose they do." He threw me a look, quick and unsmiling, and changed the subject. "Listen, I know I haven't been around this week to help you and Mrs. Svenson with the wedding. But I figured you'd understand. The pace of work is being stepped up, and, well, I had a lot to finish."

"I suppose you did," I replied flatly. The image of the woman in black floated across my mind. "And I'm sure guests in the hotel kept you busy, too," I added.

He smiled broadly. I saw a gleam of pearls contrast with his dark skin. "Hardly! They come and go; my staff handles the inn well. I thought you would have realized by now that my prime concern is the railroad.''

''Yes, I can see that.'' My voice was subdued. ''Anyway, you haven't answered my question.''

We were pulling up to the tree-lined drive of the inn. A spotted peregrine floated overhead on a current of air. Watching the bird's course made me wish I were suspended up there, weightless, buoyant. Why couldn't Charles and I laugh, be honest, dispel the idiotic phantoms that loomed behind our facades?

''I thought we'd dine together, then I'll return to work. I imagine a woman such as yourself can find something to do.''

''Yes, that would be fine.'' My words were stiff.

The carriage stopped, and the driver jumped down and let down the steps. I moved toward the door. Charles put a firm hand on my arm.

''Surely there's no other way for us to live. I don't like this either, if you remember. It's especially difficult knowing that I have married a beautiful woman, and I won't—'' He checked himself.

A darkness crossed his brow before he continued in a deep tone. ''Listen, this is hardly what I've bargained for. You must sense this is awkward for both of us.''

I nodded grimly.

''Why don't you join me in my suite for a bottle of champagne before we dine?''

My foolish elation couldn't have been diminished. ''Yes, I'd like that. It might be good for us to get better acquainted . . .'' My careless words made the blood rise to my face. I quickly added, ''I mean we seem not to understand each other very well, do we?''

His hand on my arm tightened slightly. ''Perhaps we never will. That's our fate. Don't you see?'' His words were sharp, impatient.

''I'm sorry, but you misunderstand me,'' I said.

"Do I?" His eyes were speculative.

"If you think that I was encouraging our . . . I mean, for heaven's sake," I said with barely controlled exasperation in my voice. "We both know that this is not a real marriage!"

"You're absolutely right. I hope this arrangement hasn't caused too much discomfort, but there's no other way for us to live. I'm just sorry I couldn't have a separate house for you."

I forced a smile. An uneasy emptiness settled upon me. The door had swung open for me to descend, and Charles helped me down. Suddenly I was no longer enraptured with nature's raw beauty. We entwined arms and headed toward the inn. Man and wife.

We climbed the front steps and approached the doorway, and I could see a gathering of people through the open doors.

"God damn it!" he swore very angrily under his breath.

"What is it?" I asked nervously. "Has something gone wrong?"

"Mrs. Svenson's gathered the staff, and heaven knows who else, to welcome us! I only want to drink that toast with you and then return to Agate Bay."

"Yes, I suppose you do."

"C'mon, then. I suppose we'll have to give them what they're waiting for."

Before I had time to respond, he swept me up into his arms and carried me through the door. I drew in a sharp breath. The feel of his muscled arms against my back was unbearable, and I fought to check the infuriating longing that rose within me.

As he deposited me gently inside the door, the crowded onlookers applauded politely. Charles smiled rigidly and said in a controlled voice, "Ladies and gentlemen, may I present my new wife, Mrs. Charles Whitney?" There were more applause and congratulatory murmurs.

Without warning, Charles brushed ahead of me, whispering, "I'll order the champagne." And I was left standing alone. I must have seemed terribly awkward, wondering what to say, clutching the kid gloves tightly in my hands.

The sea of faces stared at me curiously, and when I tried to return a composed smile, my lips trembled maddeningly. My attempt must have seemed like a grimace. I took a step forward and, mindless of how I moved, tripped on a stretch of train that had gotten wound around my legs somehow. I lurched forward, grabbing for something to steady me, when a bony, lifeless hand reached out.

Too embarrassed to meet anyone's eyes, my glance merely wavered on the skeletal-white hand, and I mumbled a low "thank you." Charles was at my side again, asking if I was all right, and I replied, "yes, I only tripped—" But when I looked up, my body stiffened with shock.

A face with sunken, hollow eyes and thin lips etched in a line of red so dark it could have been blood, regarded me. The dark eyebrows raised slightly, and the woman smiled broadly. Her splendid teeth were so perfect that another being seemed to emerge from her lifeless face. Yet her transformed beauty was a frightening one, and I knew at once she was the mysterious woman in black. Startled, I looked away from her probing stare only to find Charles scanning both of us intently.

Was this the creature he loved, then? If it was, he gave no indication of it. He acted as though he'd never seen her, but, of course, he had to feign ignorance.

Mercifully, Charles took charge then. He escorted me toward the narrow stairs, nodding and thanking everyone for the warm welcome. I, in return, smiled vaguely, and was so glad to mount those stairs, to turn my back on them all, especially the cruel woman who had so alarmed me.

He pulled the suite's wooden door closed behind us. I took off my veil, throwing it over a figured couch to one side of the room, along with my gloves, and bunched my train into my hand. Charles had gone over to a plain mahogany desk situated in front of a window and was sorting through mail.

My heart quickened at the sight of the room. Though the stenciled wallpaper was dark olive on cream, the room was aglow with light. Heavy green draperies had been drawn back from the massive windows, allowing the bright day to enter. Twin chintz armchairs bordered the Luster tile fireplace, and behind them, against one wall, a matching couch was flanked by identical end tables. Covering the wall behind this grouping were shelves of books.

Though the room was narrow, the ceilings were high and the walls were graced with several softly colorful landscape scenes and a portrait of a woman sewing. I stepped close to the portrait.

"Renoir."

His voice was close behind me. I didn't turn.

"Have you heard of him?"

"No, I don't think so. Though the way he captures this woman at work is . . . I can't think of the words."

"It's almost sensual." There was a tremor in his voice, as if the painting stirred him. "'The only reward for work is the work itself.'"

I turned abruptly to him. He wasn't smiling, and he regarded me coolly.

Our eyes met and locked in a frozen tableau. I didn't dare move, didn't dare breathe, and in a blink the suspended moment vanished.

"A quote from Renoir," he said, his voice warm. "He's a brilliant artist, but few appreciate him. His work is too new, he is on the forefront of a movement in art that no one really understands yet."

I tried a smile. "He seems to understand his subject matter, however. He has captured the tranquility of that woman sewing, made us feel her energy. She is focusing so intently on her work and seems to love it."

He led the way to a small covered table at the room's center and seated me.

"She does love her work, don't you think?" He sat across from me, the rich timber of his voice playing false his grave manner.

"Yes, most definitely," I answered.

There was an unsteady pause as he inspected the bottle of champagne thrust deep in a bucket.

"You believe a woman's work is important, then? I mean that she must find her happiness through her work, just as a man must?" I managed.

"Absolutely. It must be sacred to her, part of her, and no one must take that away."

His unexpected words disarmed me, and I said in a shaken voice, "'A useless life is an early death.' The German scholar von Goethe said that."

He was twisting the gold-tipped bottle and stopped. He was silent, and a peculiar look crossed his face.

"If it weren't so absurd, I'd think you were a totally different woman than the one I thought you were. Your honesty, your understanding of . . ." He shook his head and went back to his task. "No, it's not possible that you're someone else." he whispered.

I gasped and stared at him, my heart pounding. "Oh, how ridiculous! You've convinced yourself that I'm Minnie Dallsworth. How can I be someone else?"

"Very easily, if he decided to trick me some way. Send someone else instead." His face was impassive as he pulled out the cork with a pop.

The blood drained from my face. "*Send someone else*?" I queried on a thin breath. Was I a mail-order bride, then?

He poured the foaming liquid into the yellow crystal before answering. "I'm sure you know as well—if not better—than I what he's capable of. I find it amusing that you're such a good actress. You seem almost shocked." His words were full of scorn.

I stared, wordlessly.

"Your feigned innocence is quite charming, but I wouldn't be surprised if this was a trick to entrap me. And, my dear, I will not be your victim. You're lovely, and it would be easy . . ." He broke off in midsentence.

How I wanted to scream, yes, this is a trick! We have been thrust into some wicked masquerade by someone trying to play God, and it terrifies me!

He watched me, stiffly. "And yet if you're not Minnie, who are you, then?"

My painful silence stretched like a year. As he watched me, I knew there was no banking the angry fire that engulfed him suddenly. The cryptic letter had warned me: Charles was not to be trusted, he'd do anything to have his way. I had to stand firm now. He *must* believe I am Minnie!

"*Who* are you?" He rose slowly from the table, his dark face challenging me.

I cleared my throat and stood, meeting his glare across the table. "I don't intend to remain in this inn under false pretenses. I *am* Minnie Dallsworth."

Chapter
7

I held my head high so he wouldn't see how I trembled, my heart racing at my bold audacity. I was trying to maintain my composure. There was no telling what he was capable of doing if he knew my secret. Charles took several rapid strides away from me and stopped for a moment to stare out the window. When he turned on his heel and came back, I could see that he was making a visible effort to control himself.

The chill between us lessened, and when he faced me again he was distant, phlegmatic. But his words were tinged with bewilderment.

"Okay, Minnie. I believe you."

A cloud raced across the sun and the room moved momentarily into shadow. I said nothing.

He moved slightly closer and scrutinized my face. "It's extraordinary. I had you pictured, knew who you were even, and somehow this doesn't seem . . ." His eyes met mine disparagingly.

"It's true," I said without emotion.

"Have it your way!" he finally flung at me. "This understanding doesn't seem to be quite as easy as we had thought."

It was a statement, not a question, and I tried to probe

between the words for an answer. I could only hope my reply was in character, vague though it was.

"Understandings seldom are."

He threw me a quick glance of derision before he wheeled around the room again. When he came back, he picked up his glass and drained the champagne.

Then, with deliberate slowness, he said, "Don't expect too much from me because I can't give it. My work won't wait, and besides, being around you is, no . . . we've already discussed that. If you remember your part of the bargain, I'll remember mine. Agreed?"

"Yes. I'm sure I can't forget my part of the bargain!" I stammered foolishly as he appraised me.

"Good. We seemed to have reached an agreement. Shall we shake hands to seal our arrangement?"

I hoped my face didn't reveal the doubt and uncertainty that churned inside me. I reached out and his hand met mine in a warm, firm clasp.

He smiled thinly, his gaze lowering seductively. "There! Now that that's out of the way, I suppose we should continue with this asinine ceremony."

His arrogant comment caused the blood to flame into my cheeks. "If you are referring to dinner, you needn't bother to come. After all, you must take care of more pressing concerns. I prefer dining alone anyway, and it will make for better digestion."

He gaped at me in astonishment, but restrained the retort that threatened to explode from his mouth. There was a strained pause before he smiled.

"You're quite a little hurricane. I had no idea you'd be so much trouble, but do keep in mind that caustic remarks don't bode well with me."

I smiled in return, but my voice was unsteady. "Nor with me."

The contempt in his voice was hardly veiled when he said: "I believe Mrs. Svenson has ordered an elaborate meal. Can we behave like man and wife at least while we dine?''

I let out a breath like a sigh. ''Yes, I suppose we must.''

I took his arm and let him lead me down toward the dining room, now aglow with afternoon sun. We sat alone at the plain table and enjoyed, in our forced silence, the cook's outstanding efforts.

If our wedding dinner was strained, I was at least confident that I had convinced Charles of my identity. And so the masquerade took shape and substance, and I seemed to be guarded by its protective bubble. Or so I thought.

Once Charles had eaten hastily and departed, leaving me alone, I couldn't bear to remain indoors any longer. The wonderful sounds of the summer evening beckoned me, and having already changed into a full skirt with matching shirtwaist, I grabbed a boater, tying the ribbon under my chin, and made for the door.

The crickets chirped loudly, the Lester River—a lazy creek winding down from the hills to the lake—was full from rains and gushed dizzingly through the grounds and in the distance there was a sorrowful call of wolves! Oh, what a lonely, lovely place this was. I thrilled at the beautiful melancholy of the landscape and decided it was a good night to explore. Having been confined to my rooms the past days by the necessity of finishing my veil, it was a relief to spend time out of doors again. But I was unprepared for what I would find at the end my walk.

No one noticed me as I slipped unobtrusively out the front door. My presence was beginning to seem natural; there were no questioning gazes probing beneath my glittering, false mask, and I was beginning to wonder where my normally cautious self had gone to.

''Have you visited the Witch Tree yet, m'lady?'' Rose had asked me only the day before. When I told her I hadn't but was curious to see the inn's namesake, she smiled as if she had a secret.

"'Tis a spir'tal tree accordin' to the Indins. It's a twisted ole' thin' that is sacred and is supposed to help those what brings offerins' to it. But watch out fer the water surroundin' it! It's knowd as the Devil's Kettle in these parts, and whatever goes under niver comes out again."

I smiled at her superstitious words. "I'll be sure and heed your warnings."

How like simple folks to be fearful of nature's grandeur! What was probably a peaceful, serene setting seemed an inexplicable danger to them.

"Don' take my advice too casual, m'lady! Don't niver git close to the water, and tread carefully round that ole' tree, else the evil spirit that abides there 'il haunt ye!"

Whether Rose thought her threatening words would scare me, I couldn't be sure. But instead, I was intrigued. A gnarled, twisted tree clinging to a wild, wind-swept shore? It was the stuff of romantic novels, and I insisted that she tell me how to get there. It took a little coaxing for Rose to give me directions, and when she finally did, she added sternly, "M'lady, by very careful."

It was toward the craggy spit of rock with the gnarled tree that I headed now. The wooded trail wasn't long, for I could hear the soft murmur of water close by. Underfoot was a carpet of moss and fallen leaves and an occasional brilliant purple wildflower, and the sickening-sweet smell of rotting underbrush filled my nostrils. When the path opened up I saw a full moon hanging on the horizon, its silvery light chasing away the crimson embers of the dying sun. Flapping, fluttering birds were silhouetted against the moon, and I realized an instant later that they were bats.

I put my hand to my racing heart realizing that with twilight came the creatures of the night. Instead of inspiring fear, they fueled my old childhood fascination with dark forests and deserted coasts, and I was filled with a sense of mystery and adventure.

I moved carelessly down the path that exposed a vista of deepening blue. It was as vast as the sea, and as intimidating. I charged ahead and was about to clamber onto he jagged rocks of the wave-washed shore when a startling image froze me in place.

Crouched next to a gnarled old tree was the strange woman from the inn. She was wearing a dark flowing cape that fell away from her face, revealing a blanched profile. Her features were drawn, pinched, as though some violent feeling had drained her blood and only the skeleton of bone remained.

She was uttering something, but the roar of the water carried the words away before I could make them out. It seemed an eternity that she huddled there, motionless. I wondered, on a rush of panic, if she were a witch. But surely that can't be! I assured myself. This is the nineteenth century! There are no witches, as surely as there are no vampires. . . .

When she finally stood, the moon was higher and the strong, slanting light fell on her. If I hadn't known her to be a living, breathing person, I would have sworn that an apparition rose before me.

She moved her arm in an expansive gesture, and in the flooding moonlight, I caught a glint of white in her hand. I could only guess, but it looked as though she was giving the tree an offering of paper. She leaned in to the tree's twisted back, and whatever she held in her hand seemed to disappear. Suddenly she turned and stared in my direction. I darted behind a spindly tree for cover, my body held rigid by fear.

But it appeared she hadn't seen me, for she began climbing the rocks toward me without glancing in my direction again. It would have been foolish for me to run or even attempt an escape. The leaves would crunch under my footfall, and the startled swerve of owl at my movement could easily alert her. Instead I noiselessly shrank back into the wood.

She crested the ridge of rocks, and I could hear her husky panting as she came dangerously close to me. She trailed past me rapidly, though, her skirts rustling the leaves. And the fragrance of lilac hovered in the damp evening air.

I waited for what seemed like an eternity before scurrying up the climbing trail behind her. At the trail's end I stopped. From my protected perch at the edge of the trees, I watched her flowing figure glide gracefully across the deserted yard of the inn.

She walked rapidly toward the quaint footbridge at the edge of the lawn. It led to a sunken English garden. But the swollen creek below the bridge had torn away at the banks, and the deep canal was dangerous.

Though the garden was usually picturesque—the peonies and lilacs were gone now, but the primroses and coralbells burst with color, scattering their petals—the ominous rush of flooding water around it was frightening.

My skin prickled with apprehension as I saw her stop at the edge of the bridge. She pulled something from her pocket. I was too far away to see what she held, but as she moved, the steely object caught the light and gleamed for a moment. A knife! I inhaled in a quick, shallow gasp.

Her back was to me then, but suddenly I knew what she was doing. She was plunging the knife into her breast! Oh, my God! I shuddered and began to move forward to intercept her horrible action. Out onto the expanse of grass I moved, convinced that I had nothing to fear.

Suddenly she jerked her head up as if she heard something. I stopped, too, afraid of the sound of my tread. Without warning she turned toward the inn and walked briskly away from the bridge. She didn't seem hurt, and there was an easy spring to her step.

Sneaking back to my shadowy hiding place I watched her until she reached the inn's doorway and entered. It occurred to me that if she, in fact, loved Charles, her pain would be greatest on the night of his wedding to another woman. I was certain she had been about to attempt suicide.

I waited for several breathless minutes before I went around to the front of the inn and entered myself. There was no attendant at the desk, and I heard voices and a snapping fire in the guests' parlor. I moved toward the stairs, glancing toward the open parlor. Just inside the doorway stood the woman, facing the hallway. Her cape was flung away from her pale face, and as her dark eyes lit on mine, she smiled. It was a cold, mirthless grin.

I stared back and wondered for a brief moment if she knew I had been following her.

"Good evening," I said briskly.

"Good evening, *mademoiselle*," she whispered in a lifeless voice.

I turned quickly away from her insidious gape and, with trembling legs, mounted the stairs. I flung open my door and locked it with shaking hands, pulling the bolt. Never before had I slept in a locked bedroom.

Why did she terrify me so . . . ? Yes, the lonely woman was contradictory, at the depths of despair one moment and smiling the next—but there was something else. Something I wasn't able to articulate. It was as though . . . she were waiting for me.

Of course, I told myself as I removed my black stockings, she was mourning the marriage of her lover. Wouldn't it thrill her to know that I had witnessed the terror of her grief? Especially since I had probably caused it! I extinguished the gaslight and fell exhausted into bed, wondering if there was something else I didn't yet understand. . . .

I slept surprisingly well and awakened to Rose's cheery "good morning" and the heavenly aroma of my morning coffee. She opened the heavy drapes to reveal an overcast sky, chasing away lingering demons from last night. The broad revealing light of day was an antidote to my fears, and I felt safe again.

"Your breakfast, m'lady . . . Oh!" she giggled, "I mean Mrs. Whitney!" She spread a linen cloth, layed out cutlery and poured coffee.

"So I am! I'd almost forgotten." I reached for my bed

jacket and rose slowly, then took a place at the table. I hugged myself in an effort to get warm, and thought about my new name: Mrs. Charles Whitney! What an odd twist of fate had brought me here and immersed me in this puzzle!

"Would you like me to lay a fire, m'lady? Seems to be a bit of a chill in here."

"Oh yes, thank you, Rose," I said as I reached for a buttery role and lathered it with blackberry jam.

Rose had turned her back and was busy at the cold grate. There was a pause before I heard the faint crackle of fire behind me. Rose came round to face me, her face pink with the warmth of the flames.

"Mr. Whitney has requested that you meet him in the garden this morning," she said and started toward my bed.

I almost choked. "Meet him?"

She didn't turn because she was busy fluffing the quilt. "Yes, m'lady, as soon as y'er ready."

I felt a surge of joy at his summons and tried to steady my nerves. How preposterous that I would be so excited! He probably only wants to confront me with some middling detail.

Perhaps he thinks I'm not playing my role of the adoring bride very well. Or he thinks I should be friendlier with the service staff, or that I should quit asking questions, and so on.

"I'd hurry if I was you, it looks like rain," Rose said as she headed for the door. I followed her.

"Thanks for breakfast, Rose, and I'll heed your warning."

She tilted her head and looked at me in puzzlement.

"About the rain, I mean. I'll remember my umbrella." I smiled.

The door clicked softly behind her. My mind switched from my exchange with Rose to the problem of what I should wear. If it proved to be nasty weather, something simple would be best. I set my mouth in a firm line and picked out a gray dress with a straight cut and matching straw bonnet. If I dressed plainly, he could tell this meeting with him mattered little to me. He must not see how earnest I had become, how concerned over my wardrobe!

After bathing, I pulled my unruly hair back in a neat, severe chignon. There! Prim and nonplussed, I surveyed myself in the mirror. The nervous reflection that stared back would fool no one.

I determinedly shook away my concerns and, holding my head high, picked up my umbrella and cape. It took little time to make my way across the broad lawn toward the bridge and garden. The spongy grass underfoot was moist, and everywhere, breaking the endless blanket of green, were dots of yellow dandelions. I pulled my cape tightly around me to ward off the chill and stepped onto the swaying footbridge.

The foam of gray water rushed underneath with powerful speed. Though the bridge was short, the chasm below was deep and dark, and holding on to the knotted rope rail, I moved cautiously forward. Whether it was the wind that caused the bridge to shift precariously as I walked, I couldn't be sure. Then I felt something snap. Grabbing the rough edge of the bridge with both hands, I turned slowly around. The supports had given way and the bridge hung by only a thread!

There was little to keep me, and the bridge itself, from tumbling into the churning water below. Startled, I glanced back at the garden and called out in terror for help. But Charles wasn't there! I could see no one!

The horror of my position dawned on me as I made a mad leap back the way I had come. The mysterious woman had done this! She had purposely cut the rope so that I would fall. This was no accident.

I lunged at the steep embankment just as the stressed bridge gave way. I sunk my nails into the moist bank, and digging in with my boots, found a foothold so I could lift myself up. I scratched my way up the cliff, like a cat, and holding on to some scruffy outgrowth managed to pull myself up to safety.

I stood, gasping and panting, staring at the grotesque, fallen bridge.

"Minnie! What's happened?"

I turned to look. It was Charles, and he was dressed for work, in casual trousers and shirt with suspenders. "Are you all right?" he asked, but his eyes never left the bridge, savagely torn from the bank. A piece remained suspended, like a misshapen ladder, and it was still swinging from the fall.

"I . . . yes, I'm fine," I said huskily.

He searched my face. Though he stood solidly away from me and made no move to comfort me, I could see that he was visibly shaken. His eyes were full of shock and his voice, when he spoke again, wavered.

"It's an old bridge. It should have been replaced before this."

"Perhaps you should have done it then! Before someone was killed!"

"I'm sorry . . . I really had no idea it was weak. I don't blame you for being angry."

"Are you in the habit of keeping the grounds in such disrepair, or is it only when you bring home a new bride and want to do away with her?" I spat, reckless with burgeoning anger.

We glared at each other. The wind tossed through the pines. The churlish water rushed. The cool air around us bristled with tension.

"What are you insinuating?" he demanded.

Mercifully I bit back a cruel accusation just in time. I had been about to blame the woman for her evil deed when a new thought dawned.

What if he was her partner in crime . . . ? How easy it would be. A solitary woman checks into the inn, acting as if she and Charles are strangers, and then after Charles's marriage, his new bride is drowned in a freak accident. . . .

"You're shivering. Will you let me take you inside?" His manner had changed. His voice was low and laced with emotion.

"Yes, I think so."

I could not understand why the idea of Charles's involvement seemed so fantastic. All the pieces seem to fit, yet some vague doubt still nagged me, and I was too dazed to see clearly—yet.

We didn't talk as he led me back to the inn, away from the dreadful footbridge that I would never trod again. He was normal, even cool, but I could tell by his eyes that some grave concern troubled him. Had his lover acted too hastily . . . ?

I was carefully tended to. Mrs. Svenson came bustling to the rescue, as always in crises, and she made me a cup of strong coffee, ordering me to lie on the chaise lounge. It was a relief to be back in my room, safe, and I gazed drowsily at the dancing tongues of fire in the grate.

It was raining quite heavily when Rose came in later that morning with tea and fresh cakes. It was a soft, cold rain without the fireworks of thunder and lightening. It pattered gently on the roof tiles, and as I lazily watched Rose prepare the tea, a sudden idea brought me to life. I sat up quickly, my eyes wide. She looked at me with surprise.

I ran over to her. "Rose, I just thought of something! Tell me quickly"—I grabbed her hand—"did Charles come to you personally this morning and ask that I meet him in the garden?"

Chapter 8

I stood in front of the French artist's painting again, the lovely pastel of the woman sewing. There was something so marvelously serene about her that it calmed me and prepared me for the interview with Charles. There was no fire in the grate, for the day was warm and cloudless.

Summer now was in full swing. The lake was a lulling, gentle thing, butterflies quivered in the turquoise air, the fresh-mown grass smelled elysian. And the mysterious lady had gone. I knew because I saw her leave myself.

Rose had confided in me two days ago that my invitation to meet Charles had come by way of a note. "It was only a piece of notepaper with scribbling on it. In tall, looped letters, they was," she had told me. It was short and very straightforward. Only something like: "Miss Rose; Please inform Mrs. Whitney that I would like to meet her in the garden as soon as possible. Mr. Whitney."

Whether I listened to some innate voice or desired his innocence so much, I didn't know. But I stopped feeling that Charles was involved. Then, when the ghostly woman left, I felt sure I was safe—for a little while at least.

I'd had fleeting thoughts of escape, but it sounded so dreadful. I would have to earn my living as a dressmaker once more. I loved my work, but that didn't erase the ugly reality of having to live in dreary quarters again. A genteel woman, reared to believe oneself a lady, and then divorced and living alone in a room.

"I'm glad to see you admiring my gift to you." I whirled around at the sound of the masculine voice. The door to his dressing room slammed heavily behind him.

Why he had invited me here was a mystery. But I hoped the interview would be short, because I wanted to enjoy the beautiful day, especially after two days of torrential rain. Dressed in one of Minnie's rather unadorned walking suits, I planned to go to the Witch Tree. I wanted to see what the mysterious woman had hidden in the tree's twisted bark.

"Please sit down, Minnie. You seem agitated."

"No, only surprised." I was embarrassed at being caught in a daydream, and my voice sounded arrogant when I spoke. "Did I hear you say 'gift'?"

He smiled: "I did. I feel I must repay you for your discomfort of the bridge accident in some way. It is the least I can do. I'll have Fuller hang in it in your chambers as soon as you decide where you'd like it."

I felt my back stiffen. I didn't understand my feelings completely, but I knew it was wrong to accept such a gift from him.

"It's generous of you, but . . . I can't accept such an effusive gift. I mean, it's very valuable."

His eyes sparkled, but he frowned. "Minnie, whether or not you are aware of it, the painting is only as valuable as the beholder makes it. It is a treasure to you and me because we can see the beauty in it. If someone else looked upon it, well, perhaps it would be nothing. 'Beauty is in the eye of the beholder.'"

I fastened my gaze on him and said as severely as possible, "There is really no need for this gift."

Something in my statement made his eyes snap, and he stood. "I must disagree. But I don't think that's the point. It seems accepting a gift from me makes you uncomfortable. Would it be any different if this were a gift from him?"

My cheeks flooded with color. "I . . . I don't know," I stammered fatuously.

"It seems I have my answer," he said huskily under his breath, "but nevertheless I insist that you accept my gift to you."

"It's very generous, but it's really not necessary—"

"It's very necessary." His words were curt.

I stood and faced him squarely. "Then I thank you very much," I said coldly as my emotions grew warmer.

"Perhaps my second offering of peace will spark a greater response." His eyes bore into mine.

How exciting this man made me feel, how alive! As if all my senses were lit by some electric current.

He crossed his arms. "We have been invited to the grand opening of Duluth's new opera house this Saturday. I think we should go. Don't you?"

Trying to act as though the invitation were trifling, I answered "yes" flatly.

"Good. I'm glad you've accepted," he said without inflection in his voice.

I moved toward the door, but he opened it before I could get there. He inclined his head so I couldn't see his face and said thickly, "We'll be forced to be seen together in public to make this charade work."

I turned sharply and said to him in a biting tone, "I'll try to act the adoring wife."

He said nothing, but cast his glance down to meet mine. I smiled thinly and turned away.

Damn the insolent man! I swore as I fled along the shadowy halls and down the stairs toward the door. The warm, moist air hit my face as I emerged into the summer day. At a distance I saw several men at work on the broken bridge, an air hammer blasting noisily into the clear air. I looked away, quickly brushing the horrible recollection from my mind.

Hiking up my skirts, I ran down the forested trail to the water, making for the Witch Tree. It wasn't long before I came upon the pointed shelf of rock supporting the strange, scruffy tree, and I walked carefully upon the stones.

Gently, as if I would overturn a grave by moving too clumsily, I moved up to the Witch Tree and touched its craggy bark. A giant black and white bird plunged from the tree and circled in the air overhead. I jumped back and watched while the bird wheeled around the cove and came back to perch on another tree, some distance away.

When it seemed safe I stepped up to the tree again and reached a nervous hand into one of the dry fissures. What was I expecting to find? Rose had mentioned "offerings," but that is not what I searched for. This might be a secret hiding place for a treasured love note. And what right had I to come prying?

I found nothing, anyway. The tree was a dry, impregnable thing that seemed as dead as the volcanic rocks it grew out of. What the strange woman had done with the paper I had seen in her hand that night was as much a mystery as she was.

Moving away from the tree, I saw the menacing bird swoop back again and make for the tree's green topnotch. As he flew, he snagged something white from the far side of a tangled branch. Shaking what seemed to be paper from his claw, he dropped it on the slippery rocks just below him.

I lunged for it, almost hurling myself into the dark water, and scared the bird away again. There were two scraps of paper and they were damp from the rocks. I opened them with trembling fingers. The first one read:

June 26, 1884

Charles,

I am forwarding you the remaining money for the last mile of track. You'd be wise to meet your deadline, otherwise you owe me the forfeiture bond. Minnie's train is scheduled to arrive today. I hope you treat her with utmost fairness and good manners, and don't act the rake as you usually do with women. If there are any concerns, let me know.

At the bottom was a scrawled, illegible initial.
I unfolded the second note.

July 3, 1884

Francis,

Yes, Minnie has arrived safely, though she missed her near-death in a terrible train accident that claimed many lives. There is something odd—

There was an ink blot on the page and the sharp, even letters stopped in a long blurred line as if the writer were suddenly interrupted. I say writer, but it was obvious who wrote them. The sinister woman had evidentally stolen the letters from Charles. But of what import were they, and why had she hidden them in the tree?

I heard a rustling sound and glanced up warily. How foolish to stand here in the open reading these! Clutching the notes carefully, I made a dash up the rocks and realized the sound had been caused by the poor bird trying, once more, to get back to his tree.

"Go home!" I chided softly as he whirled overhead. "I'll not bother you any more." And I ran breathlessly all the way back to the inn.

Stuffing the notes into my skirt pocket before entering the inn, I nodded to the impeccably groomed porter.

"'Ev'ning, madam," he said politely.

"Good evening," I answered and tried to steady my trembling legs as I moved up the stairs. Finally, out of sight of the service staff, I burst into my room and fell onto the chaise lounge, pulling the letters out. I perused them several times before I stood and walked over to the mirror. The glassy-eyed, red-cheeked reflection that gazed back knew, as I did, that though I might be closer to the truth, I was still far from it.

Taking a turn around the room, my hand on my cheek, I ran through the facts that I had gleaned from the letters. Charles was being funded to build this railroad. In return, he was keeping the third party's woman—Francis was clearly his name—and the woman was clearly Minnie.

But why did Minnie have to be kept? Was her life endangered by being involved with this man? And the reply—I assumed it to be from Charles—was trying to say that something was odd.

If only he had finished his sentence.

Since he had plainly never met Minnie before, surely nothing in my manner made him suspect me. Although he had said I wasn't what he'd expected. Was there some hitch in the plan that bothered him? Something I knew nothing about? Perhaps I would never know. . . .

The knock at the door startled me, and I shoved the papers deep into my pocket again.

"Come in," I called distractedly.

A tall, lean fellow with scruffy sideburns stuck his head inside my door. He wore the inn's livery, and his ill-fitting suit was as out of place on his gaunt figure as he seemed to feel in my room.

"Got orders from the master, madam, that I is sup'osed to measure yer walls for a picture."

"Oh, yes, come in." I had given absolutely no thought to walls or pictures and glanced around quickly to find a suitable space for the painting.

"Over here is nice," I said, finding a blank wall that fronted my workroom.

And as I watched from my seated position on the chaise lounge, the beautiful, tender painting of Renoir's sewing woman was hung in my room. I stared at the woman until I cried, thinking that no one had ever given me such a gift before.

Chapter 9

I could hardly wait for opening night at the opera. Each day as I rose and saw Renoir's splendid portrait hanging on the wall, my feelings toward Charles warmed. Call it womans' intuition, if you will, but I was beginning to understand why he married me. And I longed with all my heart to go to him and tell him I understood. But that I mustn't do.

He had married me for financial gain, that I knew for certain. But how wrong was that? Charles was ambitious, yes, but hardly immoral. Wasn't it better to be motivated and take what one needed in order to insure one's happiness? Instead of letting anguished, crippling emotions strangle one's hope and destroy a loved one, as Clyde had done to me?

In fact, the more I thought about the cryptic letters, the more reassured I felt about Charles's character. He was hardly a cut-throat villian, as this Francis had made him out to be, and as I glanced again at the portrait I knew that, indeed, Charles was kind.

And my recent trip to the Witch Tree had satisfied my curiosity for clues about Charles's entanglement with the mysterious woman. Two stolen business letters. Not much of a lovers' tryst!

Yet hadn't I gained some invaluable information from

them? Charles's role was now emerging as transparent as a bubble.

With my newfound-understanding of things, the days sped by rapidly. I was immersed in the fury of a new dressmaking project. I wanted to look stunning for the opera and knew this dress would certainly turn heads, though I had only one man in mind.

I had enough bottle-green silk to make a heavily flounced skirt. For the bodice I used the lovely piece of cream chantilly lace purchased in Duluth. The line of the dress was rather daring, and I hoped it wouldn't make me uncomfortable. But wasn't I feeling daring lately?

When the gown was complete I was thrilled to see its perfection! It glimmered with a silver sheen in the flickering lamplight, and I knew Charles would notice me.

My enthusiasm did not last. Mrs. Svenson had offered to assist me in dressing, as Rose was training a new maid-of-all-work, and when she came for me the evening of the event, she gave me a shocked look.

I was wearing only my steel-and-lace dress improver with panniers and corset. After scolding me for my "fancy underwear," she took one look at the gown and frowned disapprovingly.

"Why are you wearing such an enormous bustle? The dresses here been flat for so long now it's going to look like you have a deformity!"

I grabbed my dress and pulled it over my head. The silk felt cool against my skin as it slid on. "Don't be a fool!" I chided her in a muffled voice. "It's the latest style from Paris."

I tried to regain some of my thrill of accomplishment as she slowly buttoned me. She kept sighing and complaining that the buttons were too small, and I began feeling like I might not be a glittering star after all.

Arranging the tournure so that the pleats of foamy material fell over the bustle, she instructed me to turn around and stepped back to survey me.

Her blue eyes were round and she said on a whisper, "Bless my soul, child! You are just too young to be dressed in so *revealing* a gown!"

"I'm hardly a child," I retorted angrily as I attached a feather in place over my chignon and pulled on my gloves. "I'm twenty-three years old and have already been—"

I stopped myself. Damn the infuriating woman! It was obvious that she wanted me to reveal my age, which I had unwittingly done already. She continued to prattle again.

"I sup'ose that's what women wear in New York and those big cities, but that doesn't mean it's any less sinful!"

I shot her an annoyed look and asked her to hand me my cape. She fetched my cape silently, her verol curls bouncing.

What a bothersome, sharp-tongued woman she was! I thought dismally as she fitted the light cape over my shoulders. Why did Charles hire her?

"If I were you, I'd prepare myself for this evening," she said irritatingly.

I whirled to face her. "What in heavens are you talking about?"

Her ruddy, saggy face came to life as she spoke. "Mr. Whitney received a telegram just a short time ago, and he's been in a rather nasty state ever since. Seems as if he must have received a bit of bad news."

She pursed her narrow mouth as she scrutinized me. "Well, I sup'ose you'll do, but don't say I didn't warn you about the master's being in a foul mood."

I checked myself in the cheval mirror one last time. "Mrs. Svenson, I'm sure Charles's telegram concerns business," I said sternly while preening at my reflection.

The deep green of the dress glowed like an emerald, and my skin looked soft against the color. My eyes sparkled in anticipation, and I smiled with pride, knowing I'd achieved the look I was after. Hadn't Minnie told me I'd be a beauty if I dressed carefully? Dear Minnie, I hope you're right!

"Mrs. Whitney, can I speak plainly?"

I picked up my beaded purse and made for the door. "You've certainly done so thus far, haven't you?"

She inhaled slightly at my response, but nothing would keep her from relaying bad news. "I don' know anything about your . . . about the marriage between you and Mr. Whitney, but when I handed him the telegram, he swore under his breath and then went into the parlor and slammed the door. I can' say how long he was locked in there, but he was sure angry!"

I turned slowly to face her, my hand on the doorknob. So far none of this mattered to me, and I was becoming disturbed that she delayed me.

"What is the point, Mrs. Svenson?"

"He said, and I quote, 'Damn woman!' " She watched for my response, eagerly, with hawk's eyes.

I hesitated only a moment before replying, "Mrs. Svenson, I'm sure there are many women in his life. Relatives, customers, business associates. If one of them vexes him, for whatever reason, well, he will handle it properly. Mr. Whitney is always a gentleman."

It was obvious that she expected me to crumble at the thought of another woman, but I wouldn't give her the satisfaction. How cruel she was to take pleasure so! I raised my chin and walked away from her before she could see me tremble.

My skirts rustled softly as I descended the stairs. Below I heard the low rumble of mens' voices and a circle of cigar smoke rose in the air. When I neared the bottom there was a unified exhalation before Charles stepped out from a group of elderly, distinguished-looking men.

His dark brows were creased in a scowl, but when our eyes met his face softened. He looked arrogantly self-assured in his dark evening clothes, and I steadied myself at the intoxicating sight of him.

"My wife, gentlemen," he said, and I thrilled at the sound of his words.

Politely, I acknowledged the bearded men, who, once we

were introduced, went back to their animated conversation about the railroad and the last load of track due to arrive next week. My interest was piqued, but Charles abruptly excused us and led me toward the door. The carriage waited for us, and Charles handed me inside without speaking.

It was impossible to sit next to him in the carriage and act as though his stunning figure in his suit of fine cloth did not stir me. Finally he turned, his eyes on me.

"You are the most bewitching woman I've ever seen, and I've no doubt you'll be the envy of all Duluth," he said softly.

His words caused my cheeks to flame, and I put a gloved hand there. I could hardly bear the high fever of emotion I was living with.

"You are subdued tonight. Is something bothering you that I should know about?" Though the words were gentle, there was a trace of severity to his tone.

"There's so much talk about railroads and deadlines, and I find myself hopelessly ignorant about it all," I responded vaguely, hoping he would confide in me.

"It's true. I haven't told you anything about my work, and it's hardly fair. I have a feeling perhaps talk of figures and estimates and plans wouldn't bore you?" He shot me a inquiring glance.

I laughed lightly. "If that's a question, I hardly know what to say. There are a lot of figures and calculations that go into making a dress, too. Measuring the seams and hems, cutting on bias as opposed to . . ." my voice trailed off.

Minnie was an actress, not a dressmaker! Whether or not he knew much about Minnie's past I couldn't be sure, but it was, indeed, safer to assume that he did.

There was a gaping silence. I stared straight ahead and could tell that he was also looking ahead, his top hat in his hands. When he finally broke the stillness, his voice was flat.

"If you think you'd be interested"—I felt him look at me in the darkness—"I'll invite you to Agate Bay as soon as we get started on the last section of track. You might enjoy seeing how wilderness is transformed by those steel rails,'' he said with deceptive calm and turned back to the window.

Neither of us spoke again in that cocoon of darkness until we pulled in front of the theater.

''Hi, driver!'' he called. ''Stop here, please!''

Peering out, I saw a ponderous limestone building with an eruption of competing detail—cantilevered windows, engaged columns and at one corner a splendid turret. Under the three canopies over the door was an assemblage of people, and lined round the block were carriages vying for space.

There was a marquee in front which read: *The Beggar's Opera*. It was a bit out of date, I thought, but imagined that even a company in Duluth could carry off the music well.

As the door was open to let in the cool night, my nagging anxiety fell away. I felt almost happy; if that strange woman was sending him disturbing telegrams, it was not my concern. I was with him now. And I had a right to my happiness, if only for this evening.

He handed me down from the trap as easily as if he had done it many times before. And as we walked toward the door, he turned to me, his eyes dark and smouldering. ''I'm so glad you're with me tonight,'' he said abruptly.

''Do you mean that?''

He threw back his head and laughed gaily. ''Of course I mean it! I seldom say things I don't mean. Especially to a woman!''

I felt breathless. ''I'm so pleased.''

He gave me his arm, and I took it dizzily. ''I believe we feel like man and wife tonight,'' he said hoarsely.

There was only one reply for that. ''We are man and wife—at least for a little while!'' I giggled lightly. Yes, for a little while, I repeated to myself as we moved through the crowd.

The evening, a desperately important turning point in our relationship, was as sparkling and frothy as the ballad opera we saw and the champagne we drank later at dinner. My feelings of doom, of jealousy, even fear for my life, all fell away from me as though a heavy mantle was lifted from my shoulders.

My spirits soared. Gold gasoliers beamed over us with their twinkling gas jets. The rich, silvery tones of the orchestra filled me with warmth, and the foolish antics on stage made me—us—laugh. We talked and gestured and applauded together as easily as if we were old friends.

There was nothing difficult about him, I told myself. At intermission he asked me about home, about the Broadway stage, about how it was to be an actress. Aha! So he does know something about Minnie, I thought as a rush of anguish chilled me for a moment.

"I'd think you'd have a great desire to boast about your many theatrical roles," he said, teasing.

"Oh, I do, but tonight is too lovely to bore you with backstage stories. Anyway, let's talk about how you like the play," I said rather firmly.

"As you wish," he said carefully, as if he didn't want to spoil the mood any more than I did.

But we didn't talk about the play, we talked about wonderful, inspired subjects, such as art and the new movement called Impressionism, artists and the creative impulse, and I realized, as we were seated again, that our interest in each other outweighed any interest we had in the tomfoolery on stage.

After dining in a magnificent eatery with plain decor but superb food and wine, we drove home under a clear sky studded with stars like diamonds and a third-quarter moon. We were nearing the inn when Charles signaled to the driver to turn off down a strip of road. When we came to stop, I looked at him quizzically.

"D' you mind? I'd like to take you for a walk to a place that's as enchanting as it is haunted. Are you interested?" he queried.

I forced a smile. "You mean the Witch Tree?"

I heard the eagerness in his voice. ''You've been there?''

''Yes,'' I exhaled. Had I a right to go there? I wondered with a chill.

''Come, let me take you again.'' He took my hand in his, and we jumped down from the conveyance.

Along the winding, deep trail, where glimmers of silver sparkled through gaps in the vaulted ceiling of trees, we made our way. We walked single file down the path until we were in the open again and the lake lay before us. As we approached the spit of rock, I hesitated and pointed to my satin slippers.

''I don't think they'll fair well.'' I smiled.

''Let me carry you, then.''

''A knight to the rescue!'' I said with a ghost of a laugh.

His face brushed my hair as he lifted me. ''Not as gallant as that, I'm afraid,'' he said as he carried me toward the leaden water.

At the edge of the jutting rock, the knotty tree was black as pitch against a coal-colored sky. The lake was as still as paint, and a breeze, tinged with dampness, ruffled Charles's hair as he put me down on a flat spread of rock.

He was so near that the warmth of his arm against my shoulder made me tremble. I wondered if he would kiss me . . . but what a foolish thought!

''Have you heard the tales?'' He stared out at the water, his voice faraway.

''About how you're suppose to give offerings to the tree?'' I asked on a rush of breath.

''Yes, that . . . and how it avenges evil.'' He turned to me, a glint in his eyes. ''It is Ojibway Indian legend that if a person comes close to the tree, and if they are a sinner, they are immediately flung into the dangerous water below.''

His teeth flashed as he smiled. ''How's that for a story?''

''It makes my blood run cold,'' I answered, wondering if he and his lady friend had met here on moonlit nights.

The soft murmur of water striking the lifeless rocks spurred my next question.

"Is the water known as the Devil's Kettle? Rose told me that whatever falls into the water never comes out. As though there was some kind of whirlpool at work."

I watched his immobile profile. "I don't know. It seems anything could happen in this startlingly beautiful landscape, don't you think?"

My laugh was shaky. "Yes!"

He turned to me then and said earnestly, "When I left New York to come here to mine, I was looking for gold. Then I found iron ore, but I found something else, too. A savage wilderness that belongs to no one. I've never been superstitious, but here there is something so big"—he put his hands in his pockets and looked at the vista—"so much bigger than us, and yet, it is us. We are as integral to this shore as this clinging piece of dried deadwood. And so I tend to believe the old wives' tales."

He slanted a look down and me, but I didn't answer.

"Do you?" he whispered, and I felt his breath on my face.

"I . . . yes, I think I do," I said softly.

He reached his arms around me and kissed me roughly. He pulled me up to him and held me there for a suspended moment. When he let me go, the water and sky and rock seemed to move dizzily around me.

His kiss was a gesture of tenderness, and I remained warmed, touched by his act, and was unable to speak. And neither did he.

"I'm sorry," he said suddenly, glancing away. "But it's so difficult! You just don't seem to be the kind of woman Francis would love."

No, I'm not, but Minnie is! I thought nervously.

"Charles, is there . . . ?" I began, urgently.

"Is there what?" He was still close, his eyes hooded.

"Oh, nothing, just a crazy little fear," I said as casually as I could.

He smiled thinly. ''Yes, there are a lot of crazy little fears! For both of us.''

There was a pause before he said, ''I must respect his honor, but I've never felt this way toward a woman.''

''Do you think it would matter so much to him if you kissed me?'' There was no restraining the question.

His brows furrowed in a dark line. ''Are you testing me?'' he queried shortly.

I held his eyes for a moment, then turned away, suddenly chilled. ''No, I only thought that—'' I looked up at him. ''He won't know anyway, will he?''

''I wouldn't recommend telling him, if that's what you're asking.'' He threw a rock into the glassy water and watched it skip across the surface.

''No,'' I said and my voice sounded sulky. I was close to tears. I had never felt so desperately happy with a man, and so afraid of the consequences.

''Look''—he turned swiftly back to me and put his hands on my shoulders—''we must be very careful, but if you feel as I do, there's a chance for us.''

''I do,'' I whispered.

His eyes were on me as he said in a breathless voice, ''Be patient then, and so will I, because it's going to get harder before it gets easier.''

My face must have been a blank, for he said, ''He has just contacted me. He wants to know when you can visit him.''

My eyes widened and I glanced furtively away. *Visit him?!* I thought, stunned.

''Well, I . . . I don't think this is a good time,'' I said stiffly.

''Nor I,'' he said raggedly. ''Y'know, it's odd; Francis has all the qualities a woman would desire. He's very wealthy, charming and a considerable good-looker.'' He laughed suddenly. ''Very different from me, and yet . . . I somehow feel you have chosen me over him,'' he said in a strained undertone.

High in the darkness came the shrill call of a bat, and we stopped, suspended, as if waiting for something.

"Forgive me. I've talked out of turn," he said finally.

"On the contrary, I think you have a right to understand. I kissed you, didn't I?" My words were without apology.

A bristling pause. "How much do you love him?" he asked and threw another skip rock into the lake.

"Well, I . . ." I pulled my cape tightly around me. "It's hard to say," I lied pathetically.

"Yes, I'm sure it is." His words were without scorn.

The lonely cry of a wolf pierced the still night. The eerie sound was forlorn, sad, like a crying baby, and the skin on my arm prickled.

"Shall we go back now? I see that you're cold."

I nodded solemnly, afraid of the crazy direction my life was following. In silence he picked me up and carried me over the stones, and then we made our way through the deep forest to the waiting carriage. The spell was gone. Cinderella was back in her kitchen sweeping again. The ball was over, and, like Cinderella, I was a woman with no future at all except what this man could give me. And that was not what I wanted.

In the carriage I sat rigidly next to him, sensing his confusion and doubt. I wanted so much to tell him that this Francis was only a phantom to me, not a real lover at all. But it was too soon for confidences.

The front of the inn was lit with glowing gaslights, and we walked silently up the steps together. Mrs. Svenson opened the door, beaming, looking at us with prying interest, and asked, "How was the opera?" and "Did you dine afterward?" and, if not, could she lay a table in the parlor . . . ?

"Yes" and "yes," Charles answered curtly, telling her that we were much too tired to stay up, and no thank you for the offer of supper, that we'd retire to our chambers.

"Mrs. Whitney," Charles said formally to me, his face drawn, "after you." And we moved up the stairs somberly.

I was grateful to be let off the hook so easily with Mrs. Svenson, but Charles's sudden coolness disturbed me more than a little.

"You must excuse me for the next week." His voice was low and steady behind me. "But work begins near the Whiteface River tomorrow, and I'll be camping with the men. It'll be a while before I see you again."

We reached the landing and he gave me his arm. "Does it matter?" I asked defensively.

He laughed hollowly and the sound echoed. "No, I suppose it doesn't much, does it?"

I retreated into my stiff, formal self. "Thank you for a fine evening, Mr. Whitney."

He bowed politely and moved with firm steps down the hall. I watched in silence, and turning back to enter my room, caught a scent that was unusual but familiar. The odor choked me into abrupt awareness. I held my breath and listened. There was only the soft click of Charles's door closing in the distance.

My hands slipped on the knob as I entered my suite. In the soft yellow glow of my bedside lamp, I was not immediately aware that my belongings had been touched. But a thrill of unreasonable terror swept over me. With trembling hands I closed the door, pulling the bolt across it with a screech.

I leaned against the door, breathing in short, shuttering breathes. There was the unmistakable scent of lilac on the air.

Chapter 10

In those moments of panic I was unable to think clearly. Only the shock of knowing the mysterious woman had been here overcame me and made my usual lucid thinking grow clouded. It was so unexpected. I had thought she'd left.

For hadn't I seen her statuesque figure, draped in Bombazine and wearing a veil, board a cab, her portmanteau stowed under its box? And I hadn't seen them drive away in the small, two-horse trap? Rose had seen her, too, she told me.

"Queer, very queer, that one is. As though she belongs in another world. Always wanderin' alone. When I seen her go, I says to meself, 'she'll niver be back, not to this forgotten place. She is too lost here.' I seen her—movin' from room to room, as if she's a ghost. Takin' walks, goin' into the garden, to the lighthouse . . ."

With a terrible sense of doom, I flung my cape onto the bed and made for the opposite end of the room. My eyes had adjusted well enough to the dim light to reveal that the secretary on the far wall had been disturbed. The top drawer was slightly open, obviously jammed, as if the person using it had been in a hurry.

I shuddered at my thoughts. "Person using it?" It was evident that my mind was shutting out the alarming truth.

She had been in my rooms—making a nefarious search! How she managed to enter without a key, I couldn't guess, but when I realized, with relief, that the Meissen tea set was undisturbed, I gently opened the drawer. I knew immediately what she had been searching for.

Letters. From the phantom Francis. I had foolishly placed one missive in my drawer: It was the first note I had received from Francis accompanying the gift of jewelry. I had burned the second one received on my wedding day.

The letter wasn't in my drawer where I had laid it. It was no where else, either. She had taken it, then. But why was she so eager to steal such a piece of correspondence?

To prove to Charles that I had another lover? How foolish, I thought folding my arms over my chest, that she would attempt something of that nature. If she and Charles are sweathearts, surely he has convinced her that I am only a mock bride, and not his real love at all.

But there was something else: She seemed curiously interested in correspondence between Charles and Francis. Like those letters I had found by the Witch Tree! My heart slammed against my chest at the recollection. Is that what she really was searching for . . . ?

Moving rapidly to my wardrobe, I pulled out the skirt I had worn the day I collected the letters. The pocket was stiff, and I pulled out the crumpled notes.

Thank God! I breathed easily. They're still here. I wondered if I should find a more suitable place to keep the important notes, but an unhesitating glance around the room gave me my answer. It would be reckless to hide them under the silk cushions on the chairs or chaise lounge. Or under my mattress. My books would never do, nor would the drapes or a lambrequin. There was no place to hide the letters in my room except in my skirt pocket.

I glanced toward my dressing room. Perhaps in there. When I lit the wall urns and let their iridescent light illuminate the little room, I gasped.

Lengths of fine material were cut into jagged, uneven

strips. Sewing needles, pins, measuring tapes, ribbons, several yards of lace, all were strewn diabolically on the floor, torn, butchered. I could only stare in horror.

"It's impossible!" I said aloud to myself.

Quite suddenly an image of Clyde rose before me. His eyes were hard, his jaw clenched, his lips pursed, in fact, all his features were defined by inner fury, and I saw him fly around my room like a man possessed, throwing valuable material onto the floor. A mingling of revulsion and shame threatened to choke me. How he had abhorred my work!

"Don't be a fool, Maggie! You can't make ten cents a day with this tomfoolery. Why do you even try?"

I blinked back the image of him and tried to dispel those feelings of worthlessness he evoked in me. This has nothing to do with him, I reminded myself. This is my new life. No one knows who I am. Yet.

Bending down, I scooped up a fluff of balayeuse and held the stiff fabric in my hands.

"It's demonical," I breathed. My voice sounded stifled and unnatural.

What reason did she have . . . ? I picked up more of the shredded material and let a piece of China silk slide through my fingers.

First my near death on the bridge, now the ruin of my expensive materials. I walked quickly to the braided bell pull and yanked it. It was a few minutes before Mrs. Svenson rapped on my door.

I told her to enter, which she did. But before she had a chance to take in my room, she began prattling about some nonsense. I had no doubt that she was hoping to get wind of a row between Charles and me. But I had no such news.

I called to her from my dressmaking room and she joined me there. At the sight of the destruction, she clasped her hands over her mouth and turned skeletal white.

"Bless my soul, child! What does this mean?"

"That's what I'd like to know," I answered rather tartly.

She began pacing up and down my workroom, wringing

her hands. ''Oh, dear Lord! . . . It's a wicked act. The devil himself couldn't have done a better job!''

''That's what I'm thinking,'' I mumbled as I got down on all fours and began picking up the tiny pins scattered everywhere.

She stopped her pacing and thought for a moment. ''I'll be a dead bedbug! I know who did it!''

I sat up, observing her from my crouched position. ''Who?'' I asked, though I knew perfectly well who.

''The new maid-of-all-work! She's a rather coarse girl and poor, too. She probably saw your lovely materials and thought—well, the lady of the house just doesn't need all that! I'll have her fired first thing, dear. Don't you worry!''

Her stupid accusation made me angry. I was hoping that Mrs. Svenson would mention having seen the lady in black. Perhaps I could rattle her memory.

''Mrs. Svenson, there was a woman here recently . . . she wore veils most of the time. She was tall and rather thin. She was here at the time of my marriage. I have reason to believe that she was responsible for this.'' My tone was severe.

She looked puzzled. There was no reflection of understanding in her eyes. ''Don't recall seeing a lady like that, dear. So many guests come and g—''

''The telegram!'' I jumped up, letting the pins held in my skirt scatter. ''Charles received a telegram today, you said. And he had sworn at the woman who'd sent it! That's her. She wanted to tell him that she'd be returning tonight. Mrs. Svenson, have you no recollection of a woman traveling alone tonight and checking into the inn?''

I held a few pins in my palm so fervently that they tore into my flesh.

''Dear''—Mrs. Svenson's eyes wavered between my face and the floor. ''I don't know that it was a *woman* who wrote that telegram.'' She lowered her voice. ''I only heard what I heard.''

''What did you hear him say?'' I demanded.

"Well . . ." She was stalling, and I wouldn't let her get away with it.

"What?!"

"Something about it being a damn inconvenient time—excuse the word, dear, but he did say it, you know."

"Inconvenient time," I repeated dully to myself.

"And that if it weren't for *him* . . . then he said something low, and I couldn't make it out because he was heading toward the parlor."

I fixed my stare on her face. "Mrs. Svenson, you told me, made sure, in fact, that I knew the cryptic telegram was from a woman!"

"Now, don't go making accusations that aren't true!" Her round, fat face looked soft as a peach in the dull light. And her eyes held a glint of fear, as though she were a trapped animal.

"I'm doing nothing of the sort!" I retorted hotly. "What else . . . Mrs. Svenson, did Charles say *anything* about a woman?"

She arched an eyebrow and glanced down at her folded hands. "I thought I heard him, dear. He was mumbling under his breath, you know." She caught my eye then quickly looked away again. "Mr. Whitney was so furious that he crumpled the telegram right away, and I could have sworn he said something about a woman, but I'm not—"

"But you're not sure?" I asked curtly.

She looked directly at me and feigned ignorance. "I've told you all I know. And if you don't take my word, well, then it's too bad you have grown so callous that you can't believe the true words of a Christian woman!"

"I see." I bit my lip. Mrs. Svenson had only *assumed* the telegram was from a woman! She had obviously delighted in Charles's angry reaction and had decided to embellish the story by adding a woman.

"You've accomplished what you set out to do!" I flung at her, unmindful of my words. "Now I discover that you don't even know if the telegram was from a woman, that, in fact, you had no way of knowing anything at all about the telegram.'' I cursed myself silently for listening to her in the first place.

She frowned and gave me the pained look of a true martyr. ''Dear, you are so young, so impressionable. I only had your well-being in mind. You see, the master is much older and . . . well, it's best you knew that you are not the only lady in his life. He's had his arrangements with women, if you know what I mean.'' She cocked her shrewish head at me. .

''Before I throw you out of here,'' I began rudely, setting my jaw, ''I have just one more question.''

It was crucial that I not fall for her line of my being inexperienced and young, as I had done before. Damn the foolish woman! It was as though she actually suspected me of my precarious deception. Could she know how old Minnie was supposed to be?

''Did you . . . have you seen the master with any other woman since you have been employed here?''

''Mrs. Whitney!'' she exclaimed, false concern edging her voice. ''But you asked, so on my honor as a Bible-reading woman, I must answer honestly.''

I sighed.

''Dear,'' she began, fidgeting with a cameo brooch that seemed to hold her overextended collar together, ''one day, oh just last week, I saw a striking-looking woman leave the gardens and disappear toward the lighthouse at the back of the grounds.''

I practically leaped at her and grasped her sleeve ferociously. ''Lighthouse?'' I asked unevenly.

Rose had mentioned it before . . . wasn't that where Charles stored unused furniture? I had dismissed searching the lighthouse earlier only because I couldn't imagine what my exploration would prove. Now I could no longer ignore the forbidding possibilities.

Though I worried about where—and with whom—

Charles may be conducting his clandestine affairs, the nature of my anxiety was changing. If the woman Mrs. Svenson saw had, indeed, been inside the cottage, perhaps it was not to meet her secret lover but to procure Charles's personal papers instead. . . . Who was this woman and what was she after? I trembled. Maybe she could lead me to the very clue I needed in order to understand how Minnie got involved with Charles—and with Francis.

Mrs. Svenson shot me a knowing look. "It wasn't your lady, dear. Though I was some distance away, this woman wasn't so tall and certainly wasn't wearing black."

"Some distance away?" I blurted.

"Yes, I was just coming back from town and was in the trap, and we rounded the corner—"

"Wait!" I said. "Mrs. Svenson, it's getting harder and harder to believe anything you tell me. If you were in the carriage, it must have been difficult to tell the height and stature of a woman so far away. The lighthouse is at the back of the grounds deep in woods, close to the water. How do you know the woman you saw wasn't, in fact, the very woman I described tonight?"

"Well, dear, she wasn't wearing black," she said with a sulking tone.

I let that comment pass. "Mrs. Svenson, was she alone?"

"Oh yes, dear," she smiled ingratiatingly. "She wasn't with *him* if that's what you mean. But my thought was"—she took a deep inhalation, her chest swelling—"that she was going to meet him. After all, there'd be no other reason for her to go there. Except to meet Mr. Whitney!"

Or to steal more of his private correspondence. . . .

"No, I suppose not," I said quietly.

Whether instinct or simple curiosity urged me, I didn't know. But if there was something hidden in a dusty old stone building that could lead me to the truth, I had to find it. Mrs. Svenson had told me absolutely nothing. Except what she *thought* she saw, or *thought* she heard.

"Dear, it's awfully late and if you don't need my assistance anymore, I'd like to go to bed." Mrs. Svenson yawned widely.

"Yes, of course. Please go to bed. You've helped enough." My tone was sarcastic, but it couldn't be helped.

"I'll let that girl go tomorrow," she said as she stood at my door.

"What? No! Don't do that, Mrs. Svenson. It will make for bad feelings amongst the staff. The shock was worse than the damage done, believe me."

She shook her head reproachfully. "Dear, that young girl must be taught a lesson!"

All of a sudden my head ached, and I was in no mood to argue. "If you must, then at least give her severance pay and the proper testimonials." Poor girl! Blamed for something she hadn't done. How unfair the world of the working woman.

Huffily, she said, "As you wish, dear. But it's very wrong to reward someone's bad behavior. Good night, dear."

"Oh, Mrs. Svenson," I called. An astonishing idea unexpectedly gripped me.

She sent me a questioning glance.

"Is the lighthouse . . . very old, then?"

She thought a moment. "I can't rightly say. It does look ancient, though. It was the first one here on this coast, had some fancy French lenses or what have you. Now it's only a pillar of crumbling stone along with the abandoned keeper's cottage."

"Would it be a desirable place for lovers to meet?" My question was calculated to send her down the wrong track.

Her interest was piqued by my query, as I hoped it would be. She moved closer into the room, and her eyes were lit with a sudden animated glow.

"Dear, it would be most desirable! Remember, the cottage is abandoned and now contains all Mr. Whitney's furniture . . . why, who knows how enchanting it may well be!''

I laughed. ''How ridiculous that I didn't remind Charles to leave me with the set of master keys while he is away!'' It was a clumsy hint, for I had no idea if there even were keys to the lighthouse or the cottage, but I had to try it.

''Dear, I will get the keys for you as soon as possible. I know where everything is.'' She gloated.

I had gotten from her what I needed without her knowing why I really wanted to search the cottage. How easy it was after all!

''Thank you,'' I said, controlling the excitement in my voice. ''That's kind of you to get them for me.''

She didn't answer, but her eyes met mine in a knowing glance.

''I just thought I'd better have a look around the place! You know, I don't want to be the last woman to know if her husband . . .'' I looked down to hide the animation on my face.

''Of course, dear.'' Her solicitous tone was false as she touched my shoulder gently.

''If I can be of any help, you just ask. Remember, I've suffered, too, and I know how cruel men can be sometimes.''

I looked up and smiled. How true her words spoken in false sympathy!

''Mrs. Svenson, if my husband met anyone in the lighthouse keeper's cottage in the past, it doesn't matter. That was yesterday and those deeds are done.''

My words sounded moral and defensive. But I had to act indignant.

A look of concern crossed her face. ''How soon will you be needing the keys, dear?''

''Oh, sometime this week.'' I tried to be nonchalant. Wouldn't there be plenty of time for my investigation with Charles away now? I mustn't seem eager.

"Very well. I'll see what I can do for you. Good night, dear, and sleep well." She kissed both my cheeks and closed the door with a soft click behind her.

The next morning's sun brought with it the colors of reality. The enchantment of last night's kiss, the disgraceful attack on my rooms, even Mrs. Svenson's ingratiating sympathy, all seemed to have happened in a dream.

Though the insistent remembrance of Charles's embrace threatened to dispel all that was hurtful and even dangerous to me, I could no longer deny the perilous situation I was in. I knew, without a doubt, that the sinister woman was acting the role of spurned lover, and I was to be the recipient of her anger. Would it be my curse, then, to spend my days apprehensively, watchful, waiting for some twisted thing to strike? I had gambled and made the wrong choice, I mused. If my life in New York was endangered, what was it worth here?

At least I felt sure that the evil woman wasn't searching for clues to my treacherous deception. She had stolen my letter from Francis and had searched for the other letters I had found in the Witch Tree, but to no avail. If she was in the lighthouse, she had probably also searched Charles's belongings.

But she was simply acting out of sheer hatred toward Minnie. I could only imagine how far the distrustful woman might go.

I pulled myself out of my black reverie and decided that the only antidote for this mood was activity. I had to be *very* careful, but at least if I were busy, my creative imagination would be held at bay. I would wait patiently for Mrs. Svenson to give me the key to the lighthouse cottage and search it when I felt safe. I would go to town to buy new fabrics, and I could even start on Rose's gown! Yes, there was plenty for me to do.

I went about my toilet with renewed energy. After braiding my hair and dressing in a fashionable lilac-striped day dress, I fastened the matching bonnet in place and checked my reflection. It was, surprisingly, a calm-faced woman that stared back at me.

It was the end of the first week of August, I reflected. Though I'd only been here six weeks, everything I said or did seemed to implicate me further. To draw me further into this web of deceit. There was a sticky spider waiting to trap me—in the form of the covetous woman.

I made one more check in my dressing room to make sure I'd picked up all the pieces of material last night. The room was tidy, as though nothing had happened.

I pulled the bell pull and talked through the speaking tube, requesting that Rose accompany me to town as soon as she was able. It seemed doubtful that another trip to Duluth would produce the *mousseline de soie* for the gown I had promised to make her. We'd have to find a good replacement for the French fabric. And how much money had I left? I wondered with a shudder.

Rose knocked, then entered breezily, holding a tray laden with breakfast. She placed it on my marble-topped table. I was pleasantly surprised to see that she wasn't wearing her starched uniform and apron. Instead she proudly wore an indigo dress dripping with several underlayers of ruffles. It was a ridiculous fancy on a day that was warm already, but she was dressed for going to town!

"Rose, how lovely you look!"

She giggled girlishly, obviously thrilled at my interest in her.

"Thank you, m'lady. It's one a' my favorite dresses! Of course, it's nothin' compared to your dresses!"

"Don't be silly," I reprimanded her. "It's beautiful!" I turned back to the table, inhaling the aromatic scent of coffee.

"I didn't expect breakfast."

"It was no trouble, m'lady," she said, curiously out of breath. "There's a letter, too. The master, he gave it to me himself, so I *know* it's from him!"

I smiled. I knew what she implied. She pulled a small envelope from the silk purse chained round her waist and handed it to me, looking away in embarrassment.

The note was folded over several times. My name was scrawled almost illegibly across the front.

It said:

> I won't apologize for the kiss last night. It was only a trifling thing, and I think we have little reason to worry about it. Don't you agree? When all is said and done, I believe our arrangement is going quite well. For you, I'm glad.
>
> I don't know when I will see you again, as building will start at a frantic pace this week. Stay well and keep away from swaying footbridges.
>
> C.
>
> P.S. "Who can control his fate?"

It was hardly a love letter. In fact, it sounded curiously closer to the sentiments of a rogue than a man in love.

There was an odd inconsistency in it, though. Why was he glad for me that our arrangement was going well? And why the cryptic quote about controlling his fate? I broke a buttery roll and poured the coffee from its silver pitcher in an attempt to seem nonchalant.

Rose stole a curious glance at me, but I offered nothing.

"Rose, have you heard what happened last night?"

She grimaced. "Yes, m'lady, sorry t' say, but I heard. From Mrs. Svenson, you know."

"Yes, I suppose so," I said flatly. "And the poor maid-of-all-work?"

Rose glanced down at her pointed-toes shoes. "Gone. She was dismissed early this mornin'. I'm glad she left, though. She was up to no good—it's jus' too bad she had to ruin your pretty material. Why couldn' she have ruined somethin' else?"

I nibbled on a roll and said nothing.

"Well, it's to everyone's benefit that she got dismissed," Rose added.

"Poor thing!" I said more to myself than to her as I stood.

Rose shot a look of question at me.

"Never mind," I said quickly. "We can spare no time if you want me to make that lovely gown from the Butterick fashion book! I don't know what we can find in Duluth to match the lovely material you had picked out, but I'm sure we will find something nice. Shall we leave now?"

Rose nodded eagerly. I took a quick sip of coffee and picked up my chatelaine bag, then led the way to the door.

Our trip to town was pleasantly uneventful. Rose had been so earnest in her belief that the maid-of-all-work was responsible for the destruction of my fabric that I never asked if she had seen the strange woman recently. I didn't want to cause any more gossip—or have word filter down to the mysterious woman that I was blaming her. For if she was hiding herself on the grounds . . . what would she do next?

It was a tonic to my spirit to laugh and talk about everyday topics with Rose. We scourged Duluth in search of fabric and had luncheon in the plain dining room of the Lester Hotel. My money was running short, but I said nothing to Rose. I couldn't spoil her gaiety at being able to indulge herself.

When we had finally settled on a pretty length of celadon flower-patterned silk damask and a pink satin petticoat, I insisted on purchasing a new-fashioned feather fan to go with the gown I would make.

I was buying my gift to Rose for her brother's wedding. I had intended to pay for everything, from the material to accessories, but when I offered to buy a pair of pale green gloves, Rose laughingly told me "you've done enough" and paid for the gloves herself.

I was thankful to her for that since my alarmingly low cash reserves kept threatening to spoil my day. Hadn't

Francis hinted that Charles would give me money . . . ? But how terribly embarrassing to approach him with that plea! Though my role as Minnie might seem all the more natural if I did.

Thankfully, Rose and I were able to depart Duluth while I had some change left. We made our way home in an open buggy, letting the wind play havoc with our hair. When we alighted again at Witch Tree Inn, we were, indeed, as cheerful and as disheveled as we could be.

I let that facade of happiness carry me through the week. I made it seem to others that I was carefree. But every night I bolted my door with the steel lock. And during the day I would, of a sudden, glance furtively over my shoulder. But no one was there. No one bothered me.

I was grateful for my task of dressmaking. Every day Rose sat for me, and I measured and fitted her. I embellished upon the rather conservative style of the bodice. I had plenty of material and, using my knowledge of pattern making, fashioned baloon sleeves instead of the plain, straight ones.

In the evenings, after supper, I sewed into the early hours of morning. It was comfort to me to work, but a sense of impending doom kept gnawing at me. I couldn't really rest or enjoy the rich days of summer. Not while someone wanted my life. Was I being hunted? No, that was too strong a word.

More than ever before, I wanted to go to Charles for his comfort. But I could not. I could only remain patient, and hope he would return home soon.

Chapter 11

One bright morning at the end of the week, Mrs. Svenson came to me with the key I had been nervously waiting for. I was sitting in the window seat stitching forget-me-nots on a piece of netting for Rose's gown when she came rushing into the room. Her heliotrope skirts swirled around her solid figure, and she was as loquacious as ever.

"This is your day, it seems! You've a letter and"—she dropped a key into my palm—"for the lighthouse cottage, dear!" She stood before me, her face gleaming with delight. "I managed to pull it from Mr. Whitney's master set. But pray don't lose it! We shouldn't want the master in on our secret." Her voice was tinged with nervous agitation.

"But I thought you had access to the keys without having to be sly?" I called her bluff, and she knew it.

"Oh, you know how it is." She was a bit out of breath; no doubt her adventure had caused her to hurry. "And here's the letter for you. Letters are so nice, aren't they now? Especially from a loved one back home?"

My face went cold. Another letter! I must not let her see the shock her words caused. I took the letter in one hand, glancing quickly at the envelope. It was postmarked New York. I clutched the key tightly in my other hand.

"Thank you, Mrs. Svenson," I said unevenly.

I was aware of her gaze on me, but I didn't meet her eyes.

"Are you all right, child?"

"Of course!" I said rapidly, gaily. "I . . . I, you know, I thought I'd visit the cottage this morning and . . . well, it's not a pleasant task."

She shook her head. "It must be difficult to be married to a man who is such a—what's the word?—scoundrel! I know because my husband, poor departed Mr. Svenson, was one, too." She winked.

I smiled woodenly.

She sat heavily on the seat next to me and patted my hand. "You know, dear, Mr. Whitney is a bad one, he is. He's got all the continental graces of a gentleman, but he's not genteel at all! He's always astride a horse, instead of takin' one of his carriages, and my lan'! but he sleeps in the camp with those beastly men he's got working for him. Haulin' fifty, sixty men a week, by tugboat, to that campsite up north to work on the railroad! It doesn't seem civilized! And when it comes to women, well, fiddle!" she hurrumphed.

I watched her beefy profile and knew immediately that I had been too eager to portray the wronged wife for her.

"It's not what he says or even what he does that makes ladies notice him, there's something in his eyes. All he has to do is look in their direction, and . . ."

"Yes, I'm aware of it." How terribly, painfully I was aware of it!

"There, you see! It happened to you, too. All he had to do was turn those fathomless eyes upon you and that did it! Oh, dear, I'm sorry to gossip about your husband so, especially after you've traveled all this way to marry him! But I think it's best you know all about him before it's too late."

She struggled against the seat cushion a moment before she rose. I grabbed her sleeve as she stood.

"Before it's too late?"

She looked down at me with a knowing glint. "Dear, you know men—now that you're married. They're only after what a woman can offer them and nothing else. You suspect him of seeing another woman, and if this lady friend of his is a . . . lady of the evening,'' she whispered, ''then he will favor her over you. You know how men are.''

With that dubious remark, she made for the door. She hesitated before leaving because she wanted to make sure I returned the key to *her* and not to Charles's desk. Bidding me good luck with my search, she finally left.

I ripped open the letter. It read:

New York City
August 10, 1884

Dear Minnie:

This letter can only reflect the severe disappointment I suffer from not hearing from you. Can it be you've forgotten me so soon? What has come over you?

I'm going to send a telegram to Charles as soon as I can. I want him to deliver you to me with all rapidity. I'm growing desperate with worry, not only for my own heart's longing, but for your safety.

Is Charles protecting you, or is he making gluttonous advances? Remember, you can't trust him. If I don't hear from you within a fortnight, I *will* see you—either here or there.

Yours affectionately,

I stared at it in disbelief. The telegram . . . was it possible that Charles had received a telegram from Francis stating that he wanted to see me? And not from a woman at all, as Mrs. Svenson had implied on the night of the opera? That this Francis loved Minnie I had no doubt now, but his harsh words stung. Was Charles's kiss no more than a ''gluttonous advance''?

Laying aside the delicate piece of net, I hid the letter in the pocket of my skirt in the wardrobe, where the other letters were safely stowed. I put the single key into the purse round my waist and left my rooms.

It was a drowsy morning. Warm air shimmered like a

mirage on the horizon, drying the dewy grass. The ultramarine sky overhead and the sound of bees humming in the flowers gently reminded me that the world was a forgiving place.

The path that led from the back of the inn toward the lighthouse was as overgrown, as if no one had taken it for a hundred years. It went through deep forest, with mossy undergrowth and thick with spruce and pine. It was hard to see exactly where I was headed in the emerald glow of the woods, but, off to my right, I could hear the steady rush of the Lester River, which fed into the lake.

I was obviously walking parallel to the path that I, rather Charles and I, had taken that night . . . the one that led to the Witch Tree. It was cooler under the trees' canopy, and I shivered, wondering why I was so determined to do this. Suddenly the thicket of trees thinned and gave way to scrubby grass and outcrops of granite rocks.

There was a clearing that created the knoll of a hill, and in that great span of space loomed a crumbling stone tower. It reminded me of a ruin of a medieval castle, with its craggy, broken column of stone perched indomitably against the backdrop of sky and water.

Set off some distance from the lighthouse, in a craw of tangled goldenrod and dry, windblown grasses, stood a prim wood-framed house with closed shutters. A tidy stretch of picket fence framed the remains of an obviously once well-tended lawn. Flower beds bordered the house, now run with a riot of thorny bushes and dandelions.

The front gate creaked on its hinge as I entered the yard and made for the front step of the cottage. There was no wind, and an iridescent dragonfly hovered on the air. What a bright, pretty day to be witch-hunting for clues!

As I approached the front door and slid the key into the lock, I trembled. Then I pushed aside my growing alarm and entered the quaint little abode.

It took a moment for my eyes to adjust to the dim light, and I shivered against the chill mustiness of the place. The entrance hall was narrow and rather primitive in its workmanship, for there were uneven, slanting floors and two crudely carved doorways leading to front rooms. I stepped into what seemed to be the parlor first.

The room was so deep in gloom, I could hardly make out the ghostly specters of furniture draped with oilcloth. Yet when my eyes adjusted, I saw a stack of old-fashioned balloon-back chairs and several uncovered rococo tables piled along one wall.

I moved hesitantly forward. Why hadn't I brought a candle? It would have been much easier to find my way. I moved slowly through the dank room, my breath quickening.

If there were any conspiratorial papers lying about, they most certainly wouldn't be in this airless room crammed with overlarge furniture. I made my way into a second room that connected with the parlor, almost stumbling over a crate. The room was pitch black and it was impossible to see. I stood still a moment waiting for my eyes to focus in the darkness. But they didn't, the room was too black.

I assumed this room had no windows, and, with hands outstretched, I moved cautiously ahead toward what appeared to be a hallway. I stopped as my ears were alerted to a whisper of sound. It was very slight, but I thought it could be the rustle of a skirt—and not my own. The hair on my neck stood up as though a current of wind had touched it. I turned suddenly not daring to draw breath. My eyes met only a wall of inky blackness.

I, who had always maintained some degree of composure, was near to panic! Why had I come here? I was beginning to think it wasn't crucial at all to find incriminating evidence. I was making the pitiful discovery that I was desperately in love with Charles, and suddenly I preferred not to know why he married me.

I turned back and ran frantically for the room ahead, which looked like a kitchen. It was bathed in shadow, but, at least, there was some light. I must find a door! For if I were locked in this house . . .

Without warning a cold hand grabbed my collar and yanked me back. A swirl of jet taffeta surrounded me. I was only aware of stumbling forward, out of balance, and wildly thrusting away the long, thin fingers that grasped at me.

The woman got behind me and pulled my chignon back so sharply I was forced to stop moving. With my head jerked backward, she seized my collar again and held me there. I felt the trickle of her veil upon my face, but the murk was too deep to see her features. Her breach came in thick, raspy gasps as she clung to me with terrifying strength. I didn't dare to move or speak. The scent of lilac was closing in around me, and I felt engulfed by it.

"Don't scream!" came a hoarse voice so deep I wondered if it were a man's. "*Mademoiselle*, you are in grave danger. And so is he!"

Her veil moved; she had turned to look at something. I took advantage of her moment's distraction to fling myself out of her diabolical grip. I heard the tearing of cloth as I twisted myself away from her. Leaping forward, disengaging myself, I felt her fall back, obviously stunned and sent off-balance by my escape. I sputtered and tried to catch my breath.

"You may run away, but I know your secret! I know who you are and why you're here!" came the sinister voice trailing behind me.

I bounded toward the front hallway, moving by sheer instinct only, kicking any obstacles out of my way, until I came upon the door. I threw it open wildly and let it fly with a dull thud against the side of the house.

I raced out the front yard and through the fence, and when I came upon the grassy plain, I stopped running and tried to steady my breath. I hadn't looked over my shoulder only because I had a sixth sense she wouldn't dare follow me. The bright blue day was a startling contrast to the frightful incident that just occurred. Slowing to a brisk walk, I headed toward the thicket of woods that would lead me back to the inn, and to safety, when an alarming blaring noise shook me out of my skin.

Shuddering, I turned round to find a vivid red tug, smoke pouring out of its stack, pulling precariously close to shore. Several silhouetted men waved at me, and the ominous horn blasted again.

"My God!" I cursed.

My heart began to quiet its furious thumping at the sight of the harmless-looking boat. I watched as it hovered along the rocky shore, a splash of color against the monochromatic horizon.

My trembling knees ceased to feel as if they would give way under me, and I walked steadily toward the tug. *Ella G. Stone* was etched across the wooden cabin in front, and I remembered seeing her captain dine at Witch Tree Inn on several occasions.

"Mrs. Whitney!" came a booming voice calculated to be heard over the whirling propeller. "Ho, there! We're pulling in to the docks, and we've come for you. Mr. Whitney's orders!"

I stared a moment, dumbfounded. Charles had sent them? I cupped my hands and yelled, "I don't understand. You mean Charles wants me to return with you?"

"Yes, madam. To Agate Bay," came the lineman's voice. "There's to be a celebration tonight. The last shipment of rails arrived—"

"And there's a banquet scheduled for all the dignitaries, and Mr. Whitney wants you there!" the captain shouted.

My brain was still too clouded to realize the import of what they told me. On one level their message made me eager. For I hadn't seen Charles's worksite and was most curious to have a glimpse of the railroad that had cost Minnie so much. Yet on another level, I was still chilled from my fright. I only stood there, perched on a rocky outcrop, looking, no doubt, as ridiculous as I felt.

But I was trying, also, to figure out how to return to

safety. Could I hazard the perilous climb along the shoreline to meet them at the docks not far down the lake? For the grim little cottage was at my back and a stretch of dark woods was ahead.

The lineman obviously saw my hesitation. "It's too dangerous to climb along the shore, madam. You'd have best luck to go back toward the inn and 'round that way. We'll meet you at the docks in half an hour." His voice had a tinny echo as it bounced across the water.

I nodded in agreement, reluctantly waving them on. If only they could pick me up here, I thought with dread, for how much more dangerous could the rocky shore be compared to my path back through the woods?

With tearing speed, I hastened toward the woods. Rushing as fast as I could without tripping on the peaty undergrowth, I was miraculously out of the forest in only a few moments. Ahead of me lay the inn.

From the lawns, a gravel path led some distance down to the small, private waterfront. I hadn't seen the docks yet and rushed to see them now. My fear subsiding a little, I started along the trail.

"I know who you are and why you're here . . . !" That awful, deep voice rang in my memory.

In the broad, skeptical light of day the words sounded hardly less sinister than the utterings in a child's nightmare, yet . . .

"Does she really know who I am?" I asked aloud to the aspens. I stopped and looked down at the smooth stones I walked on.

"Does she really know?" I repeated. Alarms sounded in my brain. A new, terrifying notion riveted me to the spot and made me inhale in deep, gulping swallows. *Does she know that I am Maggie Mansfield*?

The quick, plucky call of a small, brown bird answered, and it sounded curiously like "Yes, she knows!" "Yes, she knows!"

While the mysterious woman searched for correspondence between Charles and myself had she, inadvertently, stumbled upon some piece of information that indicated I was not really Minnie? After all, she had read Charles's note to Francis that began "There is something odd . . ."

Whomever she believed I was didn't seem to lessen her desire to destroy me, however. Now I knew my life was in great danger.

My new apprehension galvanized me into action, and I moved spritely toward the blast of the ship's horn that had just sounded round the corner. A flock of seagulls went whirling into the sky.

Should I leave? Surely Charles would understand that we couldn't continue with this charade. I'd disregarded the idea of escape before only because I wondered where to go, what to do. But if the woman had really discovered my true identity and I stayed, it was only a matter of time before Clyde found me!

There was no more time for self-absorption. I was on a wide course of long, wooden planks stretched out over the shimmering water. Two robust men smiled a welcome. One of them jumped over the edge of the boat and bowed to me, removing his cap.

"Captain Flynn, madam. I'm sorry not to have made your acquaintance before this. My assistant, Thomas Owens, the lineman." He gestured to the other lean, tough-looking fellow.

I stepped close to them, shielding my eyes against the blinding glare that reflected off the water. I scanned the boat suspiciously. "Why hasn't Mr. Whitney come for me himself?"

The man on the boat threw back his head and laughed. "Madam, excuse my outburst, but your husband ain't slept for two nights! And he ain't likely to sleep much in the next fortnight if the track is to be laid on time." His smile revealed yellowed, uneven teeth.

"Of course," interjected the captain, "as contractor, Mr. Whitney sees to make quite a sizable bonus, you know, if the track is finished by September first.'' He winked at me.

Was I supposed to know this? Whatever grim match Minnie had involved herself in, money was the key motivator.

''The Cap'n and me hauled near two hundrid men in the past week, madam. Over to Agate Bay, you know. The camps is full and men is beddin' down like bees in a hive over there. But the work's gettin' done!''

I remembered the waiter's story about there being close to . . . how many? ten, eleven thousand men? It still sounded fantastic, but maybe it was true.

I smiled wanly. ''I'm glad.''

The captain peered close at me. ''Are you all right? You look pale and you're shaking.''

''Yes, yes . . . I've had rather a scare. I was taking a walk, and I discovered . . . an old wooden cross deep in the woods,'' I lied struggling to keep my voice level.

My words were true enough, however, for recently on one of my walks I had seen a lichen-encrusted grave.

''Oh, the Ojibway or Chippewa most probably. This land was Indian territory up to '54 when an agreement with the Fed'ral government forced 'em to move west.''

''Yes, that must have been what I saw,'' I said quietly.

The lineman shut off the propeller, and a dull silence fell on us. Agilely, he jumped onto the dock and carefully tied the lines to a wooden post. A seagull swooped overhead, calling ''Ga, Ga!''

''Well, madam. Mr. Whitney's orders is to get you back as soon as you're ready. He sends his apologies for giving such late notice, but the celebration is this evening. You'll be staying at the camp tonight, so you need only to pack enough for one evening. Tomorrow work begins with a frenzy, if you know what I mean!'' The captain's tone was friendly, but it didn't belie the severity he was most likely capable of in running his ship.

I answered without hesitation. ''If you can escort me back

to the inn, I'll be ready in an hour. I only need to put a few things in my trunk."

A quick look passed between them. After a moment the lineman said, "It's good to see a woman make up her mind so quick! Let's be on our way, then."

I still trembled, but made a forced effort at gaity on our trip to the inn. How casually I had accepted Minnie's offer to come to Minnesota and escape my perilous relationship with Clyde! And now, once again, if only for two days, I was rescued by the benevolent hand of fate.

When we reached the inn, we agreed to an early luncheon before leaving for Agate Bay. Excusing myself, I left the men and returned to my rooms in the hopes of finding Rose.

But she was nowhere to be found. Perhaps it was better that way. For in my dismay I might have told her more than anyone should know. Minnie's trunk was brought to my rooms, and after packing a suitable gown for tonight's banquet along with my toiletries and nightgown, I grabbed my leather handbag and made for the door.

"You'll be stayin' at the camp tonight." The captain's voice echoed in my mind. No matter what adventure I was embarking upon, it would be my final one with Charles, for tomorrow I would prepare to leave the inn for good. I must go at once. Because if I didn't, I would have no life left to protect.

Chapter 12

That afternoon, I departed for the journey of my life. Never before had I traveled through such a wilderness, never before had I seen such rough-hewn characters.

The *Ella G. Stone* was uncomfortable and noisy. I sat on a carved wooden bench in front of the cabin, and my dress kept snagging on rough places. The wind tore at my hair, causing me to hold my brimmed hat tightly in place—or lose it to the sea. But the cool air upon my face felt refreshing, and a peculiar independence of spirit welled up within me. Even the dread of knowing I wouldn't see Charles after tonight couldn't ruin my day.

"We're headin' northeast up the shore. 'S easy goin' since the lake is calm. From there we'll take the Three Spot up to the range." The lineman grinned down at me.

I nodded politely, but didn't endeavor to ask what a Three Spot might be. The tugboat slowed as we pulled into a bustling port, which looked like railroad ties built upon a mountain of mud. Beyond the docks was a neat line of pastel buildings, a tidy silhouette of triangular rooftops against a pale sky.

It was a scene of great industry. Muscled men bent to the task of unloading a whaleback ship. Heaving and shoving, they threw wooden crates onto a gritty boxcar, which stood on a loading pocket over the docks. The cacophony of noise and activity assaulted my senses, and I was reminded of the term "boom town."

If this was a boom town, was its creation due to Charles's venture with the railroad and iron ore? And Francis's funding?

"Take my arm, madam!" It was the lineman, Thomas Owens, again, offering to help me onto the wooden dock.

He lifted me easily, and the captain, lineman and I made our careful way to the lane above the harbor. The crude wooden walkway soon ended, and my leather boots became hopelessly immersed in mud. Holding my skirts above the miserable road, I struggled to keep my footing until we finally gained Main Street.

"Ah!" I said, catching sight of the wretched-looking street. A stretch of hastily built shanties, interspersed with tents, spread from a sawmill at one end of the avenue to a foreboding lighthouse at the other. Wagons and drays, heaped with supplies, vied for space along the narrow thoroughfare.

The lineman smiled. "Whiskey Row, madam! We've got enough dance halls and gambling dens to put other towns to shame! Pardon my frankness."

"Not at all. I want to know all about the town where my husband . . . employs so many men." I batted away a fly. "Mr. Owens, how long has this town been in existence? It seems such a raw frontier!"

The captain chuckled. "Only as long as your husband's been here, Mrs. Whitney. It was a pretty wild place until Whitney established some governmental force here. Why he saw to it that lots were purchased only by permanent settlers."

"For the miners and their families, Mrs. Whitney. He brought in thousands of men and gave 'em steady jobs. Had carpenters build sturdy homes for his employees and their families. Got a regular little community set up," added Owens.

I took advantage of their generous outpouring of information, estimating that my query wouldn't seem unusual. For how many women really understood their husband's work?

I glanced quickly around me. "The ore . . . it's mined farther north in the hills somewhere?"

"Vermillion Hills, to be exact. You'll be goin' to the Breitung pit where Mr. Whitney is waitin' for you. That's where the celebration is bein' held. The last mile of track is to be laid up there. An' there should be some pretty wild celebratin' since things is runnin' so smooth."

"I suppose," I agreed ignorantly, as I felt the quick sting of a mosquito.

Breitung pit? The words sounded eerily like a trap for some wild animal. I laughed suddenly at the absurdity of my day. How could I be fearful? Hadn't I already endured every conceivable terror?

"Madam?"

I looked at the captain.

"If you'll allow me to lead you and Mr. Owens to the Iron Range Hotel, you can board the train there." The captain led us toward a grim, whitewashed building. A single track led from the hotel and disappeared up into the hills.

With wheels squealing and smoke billowing, a locomotive—which I learned later was the Three Spot—stopped in front of us with a hiss. Mr. Owens felt obliged to point out to me that the train was pulling two ore cars packed with crates of supplies for the camps, and a caboose. Luckily the lineman and I boarded the caboose, which was equipped with wooden benches and large windows. With a hurried farewell, Captain Flynn waved us on our way.

Blasting up the steep grade from the lake, we made our precarious ascent. Sitting close to a window, Mr. Owens opposite me, I was relieved that the racket of the coal-burning engine forced us to keep silent. Instead of talking, we watched the vista of untamed wilderness move past us.

We proceeded past points with colorful Indian names like

Wabegan, Sibiwissa, Gakadina and Matawan until, finally, after a four-hour journey, we steamed out of the forest and rolled to a stop at another ore-loading dock.

"Tower!" the conductor shouted.

Before I knew it, Mr. Owens was helping me onto the wooden platform of the station, taking my arm, guiding me away from the horde of scowling men that jumped aboard the cars to unload supplies. My trunk was stowed inside the little station house to be retrieved later.

I gazed around at the low, green hills surrounding us. The mud paths, railroad tracks and low line of log homes, with the forest as a backdrop, were resplendent in their simple beauty. It was a bold splash of color on earth's portrait.

My thoughts turned inward. How well Charles would fit into this thriving, alive place! Though he'd never told me so, I had no doubt that he had left the confines of New York City to be here. He was not a man to be bound by starched collars, social appearances and traffic jams.

". . . with their wives, and even some Indians will be arrivin' for a pow-wow. Now, if you'll take my arm, madam, we'll head right this way toward the mine," Mr. Owens said.

"Thank you," I managed, knowing I'd missed half of his monologue.

As we drew close to the Breitung pit, the weird, rhythmic echoes of hammers filled the air, and I drew in a breath when we came upon the mine itself. We looked down into a yawning canyon. Far below, men were furiously swinging axes against the side of the ravine.

"The ore is blasted out, madam. 'S far too hard to be chipped away."

"And those men . . . and this camp . . . it's really an enormous operation, isn't it?"

"Oh, yes, indeed, and this ain't the only pit. There's six others besides."

The words hit like a blast. Six other mining pits? The camp, the railroad, the thousands of employees? I suddenly felt dizzy standing in the hot sun watching the flurry of activity. I knew nothing of money, but it was quite obvious that a great fortune had been invested. I knew now why Francis was so eager for a reply from me. I was somehow inextricably a part of this great scheme, and Francis, the financier, had plenty to lose. . . .

I pushed my hat protectively low over my eyes. "And do those men . . . work down there all day?" I asked incredulously.

"Yes, madam, they sure do. But the contractor, he is a fair boss, as you will see. He gives 'em fair pay and provides 'em with homes and good food."

"You mean Charles?" I asked foolishly.

"Why, yes, madam, he is the contractor," he said softly, looking away. "Oh, madam, look! There's some of the ore bein' hoisted up now!"

I glanced in the direction of Owens' gaze. There was a big wooden structure perched precariously on the edge of the pit, and suspended from it was what looked like a giant ladder descending into the murky depths. Up through that wooden support a platform of sooty-looking rocks was pulled to the surface by a horse-drawn cart.

There was a group of men directing the operation from the top of the pit, and I noticed one man who stood high above the others—on the wooden contraption. I knew in a moment it was Charles. His arms hung straight at his sides. His head was high, his back straight and taut, his figure proud. He watched the ore being pulled up as the others shouted and called orders. He said nothing. But his body was tensed, ready to leap down at the slightest error.

I gasped as the load was unloaded onto the wagon and miraculously pulled away.

"How easy its looks!"

"These are strong men, madam, trained to do their jobs well. Oh, look! There's Mr. Whitney!" Owens tipped his bowler to the man on the platform.

Charles's eyes met mine in the same instant. His face was

shaded by his hat, but I could see that he was tanned. His shirt was smeared with grime, and his sleeves were rolled up to his biceps. His baggy, worn trousers hung at the mercy of his suspenders. He squinted down at me, but made no move. In fact, his only movement was a smile that creased his face, exposing a gleam of white. I felt his penetrating gaze across that expanse of space. Felt it to the very tips of my toes.

"Well, madam, we'd best let you refresh yourself for tonight's activities. The master don' wanna' be disturbed until this evenin'. You see, that ore's gotta' be ready to be shipped outa' here on the first a' September, and he's gotta' see that it's ready to go."

We turned away and headed back to the station.

"Mr. Owens, exactly what . . ." I laughed to cover my embarrassment. "I know a wife never really understands her husband's finances, but this bonus . . . er, bond that he will make if he finishes on time . . . will that be enough for me to purchase a length of new silk?" I asked coyly.

We had gained the station platform where Owens retrieved my trunk. A cloud of black flies descended upon us, and I swatted at them wildly. Mounds of horse dung had been churned into the mud, attracting the insects.

"C'mon, madam, let's get you away from here." We moved toward a row of gray tents. "Yes!" he called over his shoulder as I followed warily. "You cin buy yer pretty fabric and a whole lot more, too. I heard talk that Mr. Whitney cin make as much as forty er fifty thousand! Oh, here we are."

We stopped in front of a small tent, and Owens bent to open the flap for me. I stooped down and removed my hat. It was dark and airless inside, smelling of smoke and damp wool. Owens hoisted the trunk inside and laid it in a corner, fluffing up a pile of woolen blankets to one side. I winced. This was more adventure than I'd expected in one day!

Forty or fifty thousand! I thought, standing again and securing my boater in place. No wonder Charles wanted to treat me fairly . . . had kissed me even!

It is merciful that we cannot remain in that feverish state of emotion in which love propels us. Yes, it was true that Charles was like the spring bursting forth to me. I'd never known a truer, deeper love than the one I felt for him—no, not even when I first met Clyde. But it was also true that Charles's only real passion was his railroad, and I was only a pawn in his game of deception. Leaving him wouldn't be hard after all. . . .

"Cin I bring you a wash basin ta freshin up with? I'd best be goin' back t' town on the next switcher car."

"Yes, thank you, Mr. Owens, you've been a wonderful escort." I smiled.

I knew I was crazy to have come here. Tonight I must be cool and resist Charles's potent appeal, for tomorrow I would return to the inn in order to pack and leave. . . .

That night I stood at the edge of a glowing circle of firelight. Thrust amongst a cheering crowd of dignitaries and exuberant miners, I felt the heat of the bonfire upon my face, and the rhythm of the beating drums enthralled me.

The mine superintendent had given a speech earlier, after which he presented each Chippewa man and woman a gift. They beamed with satisfaction and offered to dance and sing as an expression of their joy. The Indians had been invited by Charles.

"Where is Contractor Whitney, anyway?" I'd heard someone ask earlier.

"Several of his men were taken ill with a fever. Whitney was worried, so he finally paid a medicine man tobacco to tend the sick men."

"Hummph!" came a dismayed reply. "When is he going to learn that you can't trust those red skins? Why, they'll steal your scalp when you ain't looking!" They laughed and laughed.

A group of cloaked Indian women stood in front of the leaping fire and began to sing. Keeping their eyes fixed steadily on the ground, their voices rose in a unified triumph of song that sounded as primitive as thunder. Behind them were musicians that performed miracles with their crude instruments. The damp earth under me vibrated with the primal beat of the ritualistic music, and I felt my heart leap at its power.

I was riveted by the spectacle of the dazzling Indian dancers who moved around the circle of singers and musicians, when I glimpsed Charles. Impeccably dressed in a black evening suit, he shook hands and laughed easily with a group of miners just a few feet from me. Unexpectedly he looked in my direction, and with good-natured slaps on the back, he bid farewell to his friends. And moved in my direction.

My silk and net gown—calculated to get attention, which it did—was thin, and I pulled my paisley shawl around me. The music infused my blood with Dionysian fervor, the hot fire leapt at my back, and I swayed toward him.

"Mrs. Charles Whitney, may I have this dance?" He was upon me.

I glanced quickly around the open, shadowed field. "Here?" I laughed.

"I don't think anyone would mind."

Without a moment's pause, his muscled arm encircled me in a quick possessiveness, and we whirled away to the pulsating candence. With precise, fluid steps, we danced around the edge of the music.

"Promenade around that track. And don't look back!" he quipped into my ear.

"Turn around and grab your male! Single file, engine style!" I retorted.

We laughed breathlessly, but he made no move to stop—or release me. On and on, around the circle of fire, around the smiling onlookers, under the night's thousand silvery eyes we made our way. Heedlessly I laid my head against his shoulder and inhaled the deep rich aroma of musk. How I could stay here! The drumbeat slowed, and a savage, primitive sound like a growling, distant storm filled the air. Charles's hold on me lightened as we, too, slowed our steps. Our dangerous dance of passion was over.

He looked at me without smiling. He was oblivious to the curious looks cast in our direction, to the small crowd of men and women who no longer seemed interested in the singing Indian women. We were the focus of attention now, and I stirred uneasily under their scrutiny, under Charles's fathomless gaze.

The music started again, and Charles said almost wistfully, "If only this night would last forever, and Francis would disappear from our lives."

Though I thought he joked at first, his eyes told me that he didn't.

"I doubt Francis could be gotten rid of so easily," I said softly, unsure whether he was claiming to care for me or just wanted to end this charade.

He threw back his head and laughed harshly. "I suppose you're right!" He held my eyes with his own and then said, "Darling, have I told you how lovely you look this evening?"

"No, I don't think so," I said uncertainly.

"Well, I'm telling you now. You're beautiful. But then, you must know how ravishing you are. You've turned heads all night. Here we are under a shimmering night sky, the smell of wind and sun in your hair, your eyes alight with excitement. You are truly glowing." His voice grew hoarse and his lips touched my hair gently.

"Is it that obvious that I'm so happy?" I whispered.

"Only to me."

A spinning silence engulfed us, and I was ready, eager! for him to kiss me. But when I looked up into his hooded eyes, he merely brushed my cheek with his hand.

"Francis will be here very soon. He wired me again today."

I looked away frantically, black fright sweeping through me. He must not see my fear! I thought as I kept my eyes lowered.

"Does that make you happy?" His voice was ragged.

I squirmed uneasily, and without warning, he let me go. I aimed a glance at him, and he was studying me under drawn brows. Oh! if only I could take him tenderly in my arms, tell him that he is my heart's desire, beg him to never leave me. But that could never be, for my life was in peril. How dark and ugly our dangerous deception had become.

"Mr. and Mrs. Whitney! You must join us at the head of the table! You're the guest of honor tonight, or have you lost your head to your beautiful wife, Charles?" a voice boomed close to us.

Shocked out of our private moment, we both looked toward the swaggering, heavy-set man that approached us. He tossed a light, round object high in the air, and Charles caught it easily.

"Oranges, Charlie! A new delicacy in this two-horse town. The Indians don't know what to do with 'em!" he chortled.

Charles smiled thinly, peeling back the skin of the pungent fruit. He gestured to me. "Have you met my lovely wife, Morcom?"

Morcom winked. "Oh, yes, indeed! How could a beautiful woman escape notice by an outlaw like me?"

We laughed obligingly as we made our way toward a log cabin that glowed with light and singing. I suddenly felt frightened and wanted the evening to end. I was no longer afraid of Charles or the others that haunted me, I was afraid of myself. My raging feelings of passion for Charles were too great to bear, and I wondered how I could possibly live without him. . . .

Chapter 13

"Typhoid! Oh, madam, are you awake? Can you hear me? Typhoid fever broke out last night, and Mr. Whitney wants you back on the next train!"

I sat up suddenly without recollection of where I was. The gray walls of the tent and smell of wet grass quickly reminded me that I was still in the camp.

"Madam?" came the insistent voice outside my door.

"Yes, I'm awake. What is it?" I wrapped the wool blanket closer around me. It was a damp, cool morning.

"How soon can you be ready?"

I glanced over my shoulder at my open trunk and the basin of water that sat on the dewy ground.

"Soon," I said, immediately realizing how uncomfortable I was.

"Okay, then. I'll be here to fetch you at—let's see, eight. Will you be ready then?"

"Yes . . . yes, that will be fine."

The blurred shadow of the man outside my tent disappeared. I searched in my handbag for Minnie's watch pin. It was only six-thirty! No wonder I was tired, I thought, rubbing my eyes.

As I began my toilet with the basin of ice cold water, propping a hand mirror on my trunk for a makeshift dressing table, I knew I had to put away the persistent memory of last night. There was no lingering over that enthralling moment when Charles drew me into his arms and we danced spiritedly around the fire. I must dismiss the memory of his dark face when I had seen him last, standing close to me in the dining room. He had looked so unhappy, and I had been moved by a stab of pity.

Then a crowd of smoking, rowdy men surrounded him, and Charles was lost to me. I was left to endure the banquet in the company of the plump, gossipy wives of the dignitaries. The boastful mine superintendent, Elisha Morcom, and his wife saw me to my tent at evening's end since Charles had been whisked away in the middle of dinner to attend to an emergency. I wondered dismally if I would ever see him again.

My toilet completed—my hair was plaited, and I was dressed in a simple nut-brown organdy frock—I stood outside the tent inhaling the brisk morning air when a scruffy young man ran up to me. He tipped his hat, introducing himself as John Wolf, and offered to carry my trunk. It was imperative that I hurry to the docking station and catch the train back to civilization for the dread fever was spreading fast, he informed me.

I glanced down the long row of tents. Besides the light billowing of canvas in the breeze, there was no movement. Had so many men been taken ill already? A minute sound, like a whispered moan, floated to me on a breath of air, and I thought suddenly of Charles. He must not catch that loathsome fever!

"Mrs. Whitney, excuse the inconvenience, but I'm afraid you'll have t' ride the little switcher back to town."

We stepped up to the wooden platform that fronted the main line track. I looked furtively around. A small diamond-stacked engine sat there alone; there were no ore cars attached to it. Two curious mustachioed men poked their heads out from the driving compartment.

I nudged Mr. Wolf's arm. "How bad is the fever? I mean, does it look—"

''Madam.'' He turned, and his eyes were fierce. ''It don't look so good. The water's gone bad, and it's been so fearsome hot in those blasted mines all day. We'd had a few local reports of dysentery, but that's common and no one thought much of it. Then a few days ago some of the men got the chills, and now, last night, we got a new outbreak. Several's dead already!''

''Oh, my God!'' I gasped. ''Dead,'' I said to myself. ''Have they . . . did they die in the night?''

'''Fraid so, Mrs. Whitney. And, believe me, they're jus' the first. They'll be more.''

''Do you know of Mr. Whitney's safety? I mean is he all right?''

''Blast yer' husband!''

I recoiled at the venom of his words. He narrowed his eyes at me and leaned closer.

''I'm sorry to be offenden' a beautiful lady like yourself, but that man is doomed, and he otta' be, too!''

''What do you mean, doomed?''

''Mrs. Whitney,'' his tone was low, even, ''he needs every hand he can git t' complete the track on up past Tower to reach the rest a' the mines. If he don'—well, no telling how much money he'll lose, but that ain't the point. It's his fault that his men er dyin' in the first place. He's been driven' em like he would a pack of mules. Work all day, work all night. There ain't no break for anyone! There's been a food shortage for some time now, and even the beer went sour. Typhoid is God's punishment to that damned scoundrel for driven' his men at this frenzied pace, and I don' give a bother if Whitney contracts the fever and dies himself!''

I could only gape in horror. Was Charles so ruthless? So driven?

''But why did he hold a celebration last night if he knew there was an outbreak of the fever?'' I asked in horror.

'''Cause he was tryin' to cover up. Tryin' to make

everyone believe that nothin' was wrong! But I tell you he ain't coverin' up nothin'."

The engineer on the train waved and hollered at me to board. That they had to meet a wagon of supplies at noon.

Mr. Wolf loaded me into the compartment with the two drivers. I couldn't let him go so easily, however.

I leaned out the window and called, "Oh, Mr. Wolf, what will become of Charles if he gets sick and . . ."

"Madam, if yer' husband gets sick, he'll go the way of the rest of 'em. This epidemic ain't democratic. But I'll be assurin' ya, if he dies, they'll be a cheer so loud you won't miss it! Good-bye, Mrs. Whitney," he said, waving as we nudged forward slowly.

I sank back into the narrow leather seat behind the conductor without answering. How blackhearted was my husband? Quickly I scolded myself for letting my worries over Charles' well-being invade my innermost thoughts. Wasn't I leaving soon, never to return? Nevertheless a mantle of uneasiness settled upon my shoulders, and grim imaginings of every kind possessed me all the way home.

The southbound journey was faster owing to the steep downgrades and the light train. In Agate Bay I was whisked away to the *Ella G. Stone* one more time for my journey back across Lake Superior. The entire trip was spent listening to Captain Flynn's complaints, not of typhoid, but of a menacing tempest that he knew was gathering out in the lake.

The blue, still skies of morning had given away to distant slate-dark clouds that hugged the horizon. The moist air was heavy with the threat of rain and thunder.

"Northeasters they call 'em, madam, and it's gonna' be a bad storm this time."

I nodded and spoke to him politely, but I was in a very far-off place. There would only be pain for me the next few days, and threat of storm could not distract me from my other fears. After docking safely at the inn's harbor, where mincing, choppy waves had begun to dance about, we made for the inn.

Now that I was back, I could waste no time preparing to leave. Somewhat distractedly I thanked the captain and bid him farewell, rushing toward the front entrance. It was with urgency that I asked the inn's eager porter to send Rose to my rooms as soon as she was able to come.

There was no reason to seek anyone else out to say good-bye, or, indeed, to let anyone know that I was leaving. I would simply tell Rose that an elderly aunt was ill, and that I must go to her.

It was painfully clear to me after my near-deadly romp with the wicked woman only yesterday that I was in grave danger. It was, I figured, best to leave in the hubbub of the approaching storm so I wouldn't be followed. There was no telling how soon she would strike again . . . successfully.

I was sorting through my wardrobe when Rose knocked at my door. She entered, carrying an aromatic tray of luncheon and a pitcher of steaming coffee. She smiled, but her face was pale and her eyes were wistful and frightened.

I turned to her, a piece of chantilly lace in my hand. "I have to leave, Rose."

"Oh, m'lady! I knew it! I just knew yer'd be leavin' us when I heard that typhoid had broken out in them work camps!"

My eyes were large when I glanced at her. "How did you know the fever broke out?"

"Capt'in Flynn tol' us this mornin', m'lady. He brings us all the news since he's always travelin' on his tug from town to town."

"I see," I said making for the tray. I broke off a piece of new bread, lathering it with the soft butter, and inhaled the scent of roasted turkey and carrot chartreuse peppered with nutmeg.

A low rumble of thunder echoed in the distance, and I thought of those haunting Indian drums I'd danced to last night.

Rose watched me with quiet intensity. "Where will you go?" she asked softly.

Where, indeed? I thought with anguish. My finances were so dire I would have to find employment immediately. It would be difficult as I possessed only one outdated testimonial from New York. Nothing good could come of my sudden leavetaking . . . except that my life would be spared.

"Well, I have an aunt who lives, oh, close to St. Paul." I began to eat, surprised by my voracious appetite.

"M'lady, cin I convince ye t' stay? Yer've already been exposed to typhoid, and, uh, it don't take so long to strike, if it's gonna."

Her words struck me. "Indeed?"

"Oh, please stay. I'm not afraid. I nursed my own mother to health when she had the sickness, and I catched it, too. I've recovered all right, so now I can nurse the sick without danger!"

I swallowed hard and the scalding coffee burned my throat. A furious blast of thunder vibrated through the still afternoon. It held on longer, for the storm was close.

"Is the fever so bad that one needs to be nursed?" I queried naively, feigning nonchalance.

"It's worse! First a ter'ble chill grips the body that no amount of warmth cin stop. Then there's the thirst that no water cin satisfy, and finally, the awful fainting and losing of yer mind and outbreak of the spots on yer skin. I seen grown men gone wild with fever and delirium. It's a ter'ble thin', m'lady."

As Rose explained the appalling truth, I could only think of Charles, for it was he who would most likely fall victim. Not me.

I looked at her and smiled without warmth. "I must go, Rose, but I'm grateful for your kind offer of help."

She looked away, her frightened lips in a brave smile, her eyes glistening with unshed tears.

The emptiness that I had mistaken for appetite had not

been filled, but the food no longer appealed to me. I tried to revive Rose's sagging spirits—and my own—with a false exuberance that neither of us believed.

We had set about the task of pulling my garments out of the wardrobe when a wild gust of wind rattled the window panes and streaking lightning flashed through the sky. I peered through the sheer curtains to witness the first drops of rain. Big, soaking drops rolled down the glass, smearing the windows, and all at once the rain fell in a torrential wave. It hurled itself against the wooden timbers with a roar like a waterfall.

I pulled away from the curtains and drew the brocade drapes closed. It was not a pleasant day to go traveling. Thankfully my trunk was laid open and ready, so my packing was greatly facilitated. Into the big, black box went petticoats, frocks, undergarments and shoes, my mannequin and sewing equipment, treasured books and on and on, until the room was bare of my presence.

When we had completed the task, I sent Rose downstairs to fetch a liveried servant to remove my bag and procure a conveyance. When she had gone, I grabbed my purse and pulled out a clean sheet of paper. Rapidly I leaned over the secretary, pulling the pen from ink, and wrote:

My dearest Charles,

No doubt you'll understand my hasty departure. I was far too worried about the dread fever to stay a moment longer. I pray that you stay well. Don't think of me—I'm staying with an aunt in St. Paul.

Yours, Minnie

I read the note twice, then folded it over. It was hardly the sentiments from the trembling hand of a lover. It was direct and cold-sounding, but I had to stand firm. He must never know my true feelings, or why I had left. At least I had an alibi. It would seem logical to escape in the face of a dangerous epidemic, wouldn't it?

A ricochet of thunder blasted violently as I stepped swiftly to the door and, opening it, peeped out. Flickering shadows from yellow lamplight glanced off the pale walls. The hall was empty and quiet. On tiptoe I headed for Charles's suite and slid the note under the closed door. I was back in my rooms before Rose returned.

"'Cin I come with ye to the station, m'lady? I wanna' make sure ye git off okay," Rose pleaded as my trunk was taken away.

I humored her by saying, "Dear Rose, it would do no good to have you come and wait in a dismal, airless train depot! You'll be soaked to the skin, besides."

"But I can't see ye go. Not like this!"

I held her hand in mine. "If I told you that I'll write when I get settled and you can come and visit, would that make it easier?"

"Oh, yes, that would be nice. I will come and see ye, too, but it don't make your leavin' any less—"

A stark bolt of lightning lit the heavy drapes, flickered momentarily, then died. A peal of thunder slammed against the rain-soaked earth. The storm was dangerously close.

"Ohhh" Rose moaned, pulling her hand from mine and hugging her arms to her.

The wind howled suddenly and the beating of the rain increased. My hands grew cold.

Whether fear seized me momentarily in its diabolical grip, I couldn't be sure, but I faltered for a moment. The blood rushed to my head, and, in a spinning fog where objects around me were lost in a hazy blur, I leaned against the doorjam for support. And panted for breath.

"M'lady!" Rose reached for me. "Are you all right?"

"Yes . . . yes, I'll be fine," I said in a strained voice.

Rose scurried to the abandoned lunch tray and brought me another cup of coffee.

"Sit down, and drink this. It ain't hot anymore, but maybe it'll settle ya' a bit before ya' leave."

My hands shook, but my dizziness had passed. With

forced control, I accepted the warm cup and cradled it in my hands, sipping it slowly. The cooling coffee tasted oddly bitter; it didn't have the aromatic richness of a fresh-boiled cup.

After draining the insipid drink, I handed my cup to Rose. "Listen, it may be foolhardy to leave on a day such as this. But even if I do get sick . . ." I paused. We purposely avoided any utterance of the obvious typhoid symptoms. ". . . even if I do get the fever, I'll be better at my aunt's house where . . ." What would happen to me, really? I had no place to go, no actual relative waiting for me. If I became ill, would I lie dying on a cot in a strange town or on a train en route somewhere?

But I mustn't worry about that. The journey to St. Paul was relatively short, and though I had little money left, there was enough to secure me in an inn for several days if I really did fall ill.

I stood and took Rose's shoulders in my hands. "Don't worry about me. I felt momentarily weak, that's all. It's nerves, of course. I am nervous about this journey, but as you can see, I feel fine now!"

A heavy rap at the door caused both of us to jump.

"Come in!" I called.

The gaunt, spindly manservant opened the door. "If you please, madam, the driver is refusin' to take his team out in this storm. Them horses is afraid of lightnin' and they would only cause an accident. If you can wait—"

"But I can't wait!" I answered, determined. I couldn't wait another night. . . .

The servant cleared his throat. "Mrs. Whitney, it's only a summer thunderstorm and should pass soon. Oh, say an hour and it should calm down by then," he said.

"An hour? But I heard this was supposed to be—what do you call it?—a Northeaster?"

"Yes, that's what they call 'em. But I can't see no reason to worry about it bein' a Nor'easter. Why the wind's not strong enough. And, anyhow, the trains should be runnin'."

"I see," I replied flatly. Why, then, the captain's insistence of a savage storm approaching . . . ? "Well, I have no choice but to wait, do I?"

"I'll tell the driver to have his greys hitched and ready in an hour," he bowed stiffly and left us.

Rose glanced at me with an expression of relief mingled with anguish and hurried to the cellar to fetch some port for me while I waited. The fury of the tempest played itself out eventually, the dramatics of lightning and thunder retreating to the distance. The rain ceased to fall in gushing sheets, and now only a soft springlike shower remained. The sky was still churning in the southeast, however, and I wondered what the angry clouds meant. And then a greater, more menacing threat arose—the wind.

The driver was evidently nonplussed by the rising wind since the manservant called for me, true to his word, within the hour. The horses had been hitched, my trunk stowed under the box, and finally I was tucked warmly into the landau, the driver clutching at the reins. Rose and I bid our final farewells to each other, and the carriage lurched forward.

Rain streamed to the ground at the edges of the inn, where it cascaded from the slanting roof. Through the coach windows, I glanced back at the timber-and-stone inn, swallowing down the deep regret and misgivings that seized me.

It didn't take long to make our way to the station, in spite of the rutted mud roads. I was let off, without more adieu from the driver than the tip of his bowler and, when I descended the carriage, was glad to see that only a fine mist hovered on the air.

My trunk was stowed inside the depot's double doors, and when I entered the cavernous lobby an eerie silence met me. There were no more than a handful of people, dressed in impeccable city clothes, fetching their luggage and hurrying about their business.

I made my way to the only open ticket window. When I

peered through the steel bars the guard waved me away. "Station's closin', madam. Last train jus' arrived from St. Paul, and no more's goin' out today. We'll be open tomorrow mornin' for business again."

I clutched the counter's edge. "Closed?" I exhaled raggedly. "But why?"

"We've got warnings of a monster storm headin' this way. We're too close the shore to take any chances. So we're closin'," he said through pale lips.

I reached for my tight collar in an effort to unbutton the top button. It was suddenly too hot, and I began to reel with an engulfing dizziness. I inhaled deeply trying to steady myself.

There was a small commotion. The guard left his window and came around to me. A lady traveler offered me a glass of water. I was helped onto one of the wooden benches and fanned gently.

"I felt faint . . . but I'll be fine. The surprise of not being able to catch a train to visit my aunt overwhelmed me for a moment, but I'll be all right," I lied.

Once I had recovered sufficiently, the lady disappeared, but the guard remained, staring at me through his monocle. "Say, aren't you . . . aren't you Mrs. Whitney? Married to Mr. Charles Whitney?"

I sat tall, my head throbbing. "Yes, I am. You see, I've been wanting to visit my au—"

My agitated explanation must have seemed as ridiculous to him as it did to me for he interrupted and said, "Why, someone's been here and asking about you. Just a few moments ago. I'm surprised he didn't see you entering the station."

"A man?" I gasped. "Who was it?"

"Some good-looking chap dressed in a navy reefer with a walking cane and gloves. He was sure rich because, well, he tipped me a five-spot and thanked me twice. Such a gentleman he was!"

I gulped and could feel the blood rushing in my ears. "He . . . why did he tip you?"

"'Cause I told him where the Duluth and Iron Range Railroad offices are located. Said he had some urgent business to attend to before visitin' you and Mr. Whitney."

"Oh, my God!" I gripped the arm of the bench and stood on weakened legs. "Did . . . did he say who he was? What was his name?"

"I don't rightly remember catching his name, madam. But he seemed most eager to see you; he said he'd traveled a long way—"

"From New york? Had he come from New York?"

"Well, I don't think he said, just that he come a long way and was most eager—"

"Tell me, quickly. Did he say anything else? Is he coming to Witch Tree Inn after his meet . . . meeting?"

I had no doubt that this stranger was Francis, and my heart exploded in my chest at the thought of meeting this dastardly man.

"Not right away, I shouldn't think," came the guard's reply. "You see, I tol' him that the restaurant in the Grant Hotel would still be serving late lunch. He said he was famished and that a small steak and tumbler of ale would do him nicely." He grinned broadly.

"He was going to eat lunch in town?" My eyes were wide; my breathing came in uneven gasps.

The guard shot me a bewildered look. "Well, I don' know his *exact* movements, mind you, Mrs. Whitney, but I tol' him that them are sure mean-looking clouds hanging in the sky. That it might be best to wait a spell before goin' to Witch Tree Inn. I know it ain't much of a drive, but darn! that road is so narrow and rutted with potholes. It's just too dangerous to travel in a storm. He'd best be . . ."

While the guard rambled, my mind whirled in a hundred directions. There were no trains leaving today, so I could stay no longer at the station. *I must hide somewhere*! I told myself uneasily. At least until I could catch the first train in the morning.

I couldn't check into a hotel in town. Not only would my presence seem peculiar without my husband, but it would be easy for Francis to discover who I was. No, it was far too perilous to risk staying in town.

An idea was hovering at the edge of my brain, but it seemed so fantastically simple that I couldn't believe it might work. Still . . .

What if I returned to the inn? I could catch a cab and, with any luck, beat the second storm. And, of course, beat Francis. It would seem logical that since the trains were canceled I would have to stay one more night. Feigning illness and fatigue, I could instruct Rose that I would see no visitors. If only the mysterious lady would try nothing tonight, I would be all right. And in the morning I would leave. . . .

"Madam! Where are you going?"

I didn't answer. My new resolution calmed my beating heart, and I moved, instinctively, toward the wood-and-brass door. A square of umber sky was illuminated against the dark outline of the door frame. Oblivious to my trunk, which was still stowed against the wall, I moved out into the thunder-filled day.

A gust of wet wind tugged at my skirts and almost tore my hat from my head. A jagged pitchfork of lightning flashed threateningly across the billowing green clouds. The only cab in sight was pulling away to the quick switch of reins and the holler of its driver.

I stood a moment, thinking. Could I make it back to the inn on foot? I would have to hurry, but I knew the road well, and it wasn't too far. . . .

I didn't waver long before I found myself moving rapidly along my way. Down the muddy, manure-filled lane I hurried, gaining speed as the whistling wind at my back prodded me onward. The black, seething water to my right was whipped into a churning caldron, as if a giant hand stirred it. Electric flashes of light danced around me followed by peals of clapping thunder.

The soaking rain began to fall again. Huge vertical sheets of water. I tried to run now. Damn my foolishness for not realizing it was going to pour again so soon! I cursed angrily.

My drenched skirts were heavy, and my feet kept floundering in the sucking mud. But leaning forward, I was half-running, half-trotting, as if I had gained momentum and couldn't stop. On and on . . . I panted, the rain streamed so heavily down my face I could hardly see, but I was spurred on by some inner voice.

Mercifully there was no traffic on the road, for if I had to keep darting furtive glances over my shoulder on the lookout for Francis I could hardly keep up my rapid pace! After a while I rounded a curve in the road not far from the inn. I'm getting close, I thought with optimism and hope.

My side ached and my head began to pound with every step I took. It was hard to think at all now, except to wish for warmth and safety and relief from the tearing abdominal pain and my throbbing headache. But at least I was almost there!

I lurched ahead, recklessly, without sure footing, then I heard the unmistakable pounding of horses' hooves and the squeak of wheels. I cast a terrified look behind me and, in the dim yellowish light, saw a black coach drawn by two drenched, skinny beasts round the corner and head straight for me.

I must disappear fast, I thought frantically, before the cab draws next to me!

I darted a wild look about me. Up to my left, through the twisting drive of beeches and pines that crowded its borders, was the inn. To my right, beyond the green forest and secret pathways, was the churning water . . . and the Witch Tree.

As intuitive as an animal following a spoor, I turned to my right, dashing behind a tree for cover. Hidden in the dark woods, I peered out and saw, with ghastly horror, that the buggy had stopped . . . not more than several feet from where I crouched! *Had Francis seen me, then*?

Before I could pull back into the darkened brush, I caught a glimpse of his face through the window. The frenzied gaze that wildly searched the trees for me was so loathsome it was a threatening act in itself. I shuddered.

There was no doubt that he had seen me on the road, and as he descended the carriage, I knew that he was coming after me! *But what had prompted him to be so vengeful*? Was he already aware of my identity switch? After all, I told myself, I hadn't answered his letters. . . .

To my utter terror he shouted over the railing wind, "Driver! Take my luggage to the inn! And make haste! I must rescue that poor young lady before she catches her death!"

The driver yelled to his horses and the cab sped away. My breathing seemed to stop, and my back stiffened as I sat still as a hare. Slicing at the riot of greenery with his cane, Francis came trampling along the edge of the path, close, very close to where I sat. If I didn't move—

Stealthily as a feline, I backed up and made my way farther along the trail. Retreating into the wood, I was grateful for the howling wind and the flaying, shaking trees all around us, for it would be difficult to follow me in the storm. Faster and faster, I rushed. All the while thinking that this man would be highly dangerous if he got his hands on me.

As I neared the coast, I heard the chilling roar of the lake. Finally I stopped at the edge of the treeline, near the water, in order to position myself where I would be hidden from him. I was convinced that I had, perhaps, already lost him. If only he would give up and go back.

"Madam! Madam!" His booming voice was just behind me! Where had he come from so suddenly? I trembled convulsingly. I was trapped between him and the storm-tossed lake!

How he had followed me so far, I couldn't guess, but now I had to find a way to rush past him and make for the trail leading out of the woods. There was no escaping through the deep woods—it was thick with peaty moss and undergrowth, and was ominously dark. I would have to find a way to dodge him.

Or maybe he wouldn't see me if I stayed immobile. . . . Straining, with all senses alert, I felt my hands sink deeper into spongy earth as it gave way a little. A black spider as large as a silver dollar appeared on the back of my hand. I jumped impulsively, and Francis saw me.

I leaped up and darted toward the water. I know this shore well, maybe I can still save myself! I thought wildly. Most of the rocks are round and slippery. If I can make my way to the far shore where the rocks are flat, I can regain footing and dash back to the trail, while he flounders. . . .

Out onto the outcropping of rocks I scrambled, only to witness the fury of the raging lake. The wind roared relentlessly, and my wet skirts flapped against my legs heedlessly. A crash like thunder burst against the rocks, and a wall of white foam rose up and drenched me in its frigid spray. I recoiled with a scream.

Francis abruptly seized me from behind and held me firmly in an iron grip. I was so terrified that, for a moment, I was rendered helpless. Then his footing failed, and as he regained his stance, I jerked lose with manic strength.

As I turned away from him, I saw that his face was eerily like Charles', yet strangely different. The hard angles of jaw and chin were similar, but under sandy lashes the brown eyes were harder, unforgiving. His shrewd mouth was downturned, and he leered at me with predatory obsession.

He lunged for me again but wasn't near enough to hold on to the slippery fabric of my blouse. I almost fell backward at his attack, but regained my footing.

"You're not Minnie!" he ground out above the terrible roar.

I shook my head helplessly, trying to inch my way away from him.

"Where the hell is she!? What have you two done to her? I might have known something would happen!" His words were hard bursts of sound against the shrieking wind.

"So you're Francis." I cried with trembling certainty, my words lost in the storm.

"Speak up, you fool! I can't hear you! Where in God's name is Minnie?"

I was so paralyzed with fright I could merely shake my head foolishly. He was backing me toward the Witch Tree, and unless I could change course, I was cornered!

A bolt of lightning lit the gloom in an appalling instant as Francis suddenly leapt toward me—and slipped, as I had hoped, on the rocks. His hands outstretched menacingly, he grasped hopelessly at the wizened bark of the Witch Tree. A dangerous wave lapped upon the slick incline of rock where Francis fumbled—and took him with it.

I stared in hideous disbelief as the convulsing water swallowed him. Sobbing with frenzied fear, I watched for a sign of him. But there was no waving arm or gulping yell for help. He was lost forever to the great, black waves. I gasped and made for the crowded trees. Suddenly nothing was as it should be. Seething water and churning sky became one, and I lost remembrance of how I made my way safely back to the inn.

Chapter 14

The next days passed for me in a submerged, dreamlike state. While the wind eventually blew itself out and a deathly calm fell over the land, I lay in bed in a drowsy, indolent condition verging on madness. I slumbered fitfully and dreamt of the mysterious lady's terrifying bony hands touching my face, their cool fingertips touching my throat, feeling my wrists. . . .

My body shivered and my heart pounded as if I were gripped in a fit of ague. And my life force seemed imprisoned within me—as if it beat impotently against closed doors to be released. I had the vague notion that I was dying.

Each time I began to resurface and feel strength flow in my veins, I was repeatedly fed a nasty, acidic liquid, and I would sink, once again, into a languorous stupor.

I dreamt repeatedly of Francis's terrifying plummet to death . . . the churning water, the threatening sky. And I wondered dimly if anyone but me knew his fate. For no one else had been near when he was washed away. Again and again the demonic manifestation of his grim face appeared before my mind's eye, and a paralytic feeling washed over me.

I was having one of the loathsome nightmares when Rose finally roused me to a waking state.

Screaming in my sleep, trying to run from Francis, I was rendered powerless, and I was stuck in place. . . .

"No! No, you mustn't! You—"

"M'lady! M'lady! Ye must wake up! Can ye hear me? Can ye hear me?" There was the unmistakable edge of terror in her voice.

My dream ebbed as Rose's voice got shriller.

"M'lady, yer've been so sick! Can you open yer eyes? Please!"

My eyelids fluttered open, and a great, burning light assaulted me. It took a moment to focus on the objects before me, but soon I recognized the familiar furnishings of my suite. The brocade curtains were closed, but an invading gleam glowed around their edges.

With the strength of an invalid, I touched Rose's sleeve. "What . . . what happened? Is everything all right?"

What "everything" pertained to, I couldn't be sure. The horrible reality of my situation could not be made better, of that I was sure. Only . . . I wanted my life to be neat and tidy and secure.

"Oh! m'lady, y'er awake! Y'er awake! Thank God!"

Rose's sweet, cheerful face gazed down at me. Tears fell from her eyes and splashed on my cheek. She dabbed at her eyes with a handkerchief. Her starched cap, stiff apron and lined hands all were reminders of kindness and gentleness, and I was comforted.

"It's been a long time—too long. And I was so worried that ye'd niver git well! Oh, but yer safe, yer well! Oh, m'lady . . ." Her voice was filled with emotion, and she began to cry softly.

I reached a weak hand to her. "Thank you, Rose. You did it. You restored my life. My God, what a wretched illness!"

She smiled through glistening tears. "I'm so happy, m'lady. Only one thin' cin make me happier, and that is if we cin keep *him* from dyin', then we'll be—"

I gave a sharp gasp and burst out, "He? Who? Who back to health?"

Rose smiled and patted my hand. "Mr. Whitney, of course, dear. He's been ill for several days now. Come home after the ter'ble task of buildin' that darn railroad and practi'cly fell on his face."

I exhaled and said raggedly, "Oh, of course! Who else would you be nursing?"

Rose shot me a curious look, then produced a cup of tepid tea and held it to my lips. "Here, m'lady, drink this."

"How is he? Will he be all right?"

"Don' rightly know, m'lady. I mus' go to him now. He'll need me. The cook's makin' a mustard plaster, and I'll apply that. He's got the awful red spots, m'lady. You niver had em, you niver got the spots. I don' know why."

"Rose, when he returned from the mines, did he . . . was he alone?" I grasped her hand in a desperate grip.

"Why, yes. Only the captin what brung you brung him, too. Captin Flynn, that is. He tol' me the camp is ragin' with the fever. Men is goin' mad with the delirium, screaming and dying like flies. He tol' me it's not a sight for no man or lady to behold!"

I loosened my grip on her. "And no one has come to pay a visit to Charles?"

The question must have jolted Rose, for she held my hand again and frowned at me. It must have seemed unusual to be preoccupied with Charles's social calls when he lay in so desperate a condition, but I was still afraid. Afraid that Francis was still alive and would pay Charles a visit. Had Minnie's lover really died in the storm, or was that another hallucination caused by my fever . . . ?

"M'lady, no one dares to visit him! Not while he got typhoid!"

Suddenly an idea dawned on me. "Rose, has anyone . . . were there any casualties on the lake the night of the storm?" I asked with a shudder. Had Francis's body been found? Brought in as an unidentified sailor?

"Yes, I believe so. Captin Flynn reported that one of his

tugs was sunk. It was ter'ble. Just eaten up by the giant waves. Lost near to a dozen men that night.''

Did that mean, then, that no one had seen Francis except me? The grisly realization made my blood run cold. Would I be accused, then, of his death if he was found . . . ? Or was he lost forever? For he was drowned in the inexplicable whirlpool next to Witch Tree. . . .

''It was awful. The fever, the storm, all in the same night!'' Rose continued. ''Why, when you come home that night, drenched and delirious with fever, most the servants left. They run home for fear of catchin' the awful disease. I tol' em that I could nurse ye back to health singlehandedly, but that didn' stop 'em from runnin.' Mrs. Svenson was the first to go. She said there wasn't much she could do, anyway.''

I smiled at the idea of Mrs. Svenson's leaving.

''The cook, she wasn't afraid, so she stayed on, along with a few guests. But though I tol' everyone I could take care of ye alone, I did have help nursin' ye.'' Rose shot me a sheepish glance.

I clutched her wrist. ''You had someone else nursing me? Was it cook?''

''Nooo.'' She stood to face me fully. ''It wasn't cook . . .'' She was stalling, and I couldn't imagine why she hesitated.

''Who?'' I demanded.

''M'lady, y'er not gonna' like this, but I, well, the lady with the veil, the one that left about a month ago. The lady I said would niver return?'' She smiled nervously. ''Well, she come back! M'lady? Are you all right?''

The blood rushed into my head as I grappled with what Rose told me. Why I was so incredulous at the mysterious woman's behavior I really couldn't say. For I knew she would return, knew she would try to end my life as swiftly as possible. Yet I shuddered miserably. Again she had failed in her terrible deed.

''She offered to help me, and, oh, m'lady! I so desperately needed assistance. Everyone else had fled. Even the doctor was no help. I thought I could nurse ye alone, but ye was so sick, and then the lady offered to give ye some black potent, called Old Blacky, and she said it would work like magic—''

''*You let her give me some sort of nostrum*?'' I whispered.

''Yes, m'lady, I'm 'fraid so. But, oh, forgive me, I didn't know what else to do!'' Her brows creased and she began ringing her hands piteously. ''Ye was so sick, and I was beyond myself! So I let her give you some. And, see! ye recovered.''

Yes, I thought grimly, only by the grace of God. That sensation of rising to consciousness, then being given a draught of acidic liquid and falling back into a cloudy stupor. The dreams of cold, bony hands touching my face, those grotesque nightmares . . . They were not dreams at all, but reality! I had no doubt that Old Blacky might contain morphine . . . or even opium.

''Is she still here?'' I asked woodenly.

''What?''

''I said where is she? Has she left?''

''Yes, she's gone now. She left jus' yesterday mornin'. Ye see, when the master come home with the typhoid fever, I took the bottle and tried givin' Mr. Whitney some of the medicine. I thought maybe it'd make 'em better, like it done ye. That lady—you know she niver tol' me her name, and she had a real thick accent from the continent—was jus' leavin', and when she couldn' find the bottle, she got real anxious and come runnin' into the master's chamber and tol' me to stop!''

I stared at her in disbelief. The woman had obviously panicked when she thought Rose was giving her lover the poison draught!

''Then, m'lady, she jus' took the bottle and left!''

I closed my eyes wearily. ''Thank God you didn't give Charles any,'' I sighed.

Rose peered at me anxiously from under her white cotton mob-cap. "Yes . . ."

There was a moment of dizzying silence. Then Rose asked timidly, "Will ye be all right, m'lady? I have to return to Mr. Whitney now—"

I pushed myself away from the pillows. "Yes, you must go to him!"

Charles must live, I thought desperately! And when he recovers, he must never know I had seen Francis. Francis would only be another casualty of the frightful storm.

"What about Dr. Clemens?" I queried anxiously. "Surely the doctor could be called in to treat Charles."

"There is no way that man is gonna' come out here! He spent the better half a' last week in the camps, and now he's got the fever himself. It'll be God's mercy if he pulls through at his age."

"Oh," I said, and it was more a strangled sob than a sigh.

"Mr. Whitney's in the grip of chills and tremors," Rose informed me.

I was pulling down the quilt with trembling hands and trying to sit up when Rose stopped me. There was nothing else to do but go to Charles and take care of him.

"You'll not be any help to me in your condition! I cin handle him alone, and if I need help, well . . ." She swallowed her words, and I was struck at her suddenly vague manner.

It took me less than an hour to wash and dress after Rose left me. Thank heavens someone had brought my trunk to the inn for me! And I had no doubt it was Rose who made sure my dresses were hung neatly in the wardrobe.

Several times I paused in my dressing, gripped by a weakness so debilitating I could hardly move. I was terrifyingly weak and felt only a few degrees this side of faintness, but I wasn't discouraged. Thankfully Rose had left me smelling salts, and I used them more than once.

As I pulled by hair back with silver combs and rolled up the cotton sleeves of my plain frock, I was full of passionate purpose. Whatever condition Charles was in, I must make him well again!

When I entered his gloomy bedroom, a pungent, sharp scent of body odor that was unnatural to Charles stung my nostrils. The velvet drapes had been pulled closed, and littered about the floor were bunches of wet linen and towels tossed carelessly aside. In the room's center, lying prostrate on the four-poster, was Charles. He tossed his head from side to side with his eyes closed and his face contorted. A patchwork quilt was flung in a slovenly manner over his legs. His starched shirt had been ripped open and it clung damply to his skin; his heaving chest was exposed. Peppered about his torso and face were fine little red marks, as though he had been bitten by mosquitoes. I ran to the bed and bent over him.

His eyes opened for a moment, and the steel-gray irises were glassy, the whites red and congested. "You're not her! I told you not to stay. It's dangerous! Get out!" His voice was thick, his words slurred.

I swayed back at the ferocity of his words. Without warning, Rose rushed up behind me, grabbing my arm, jerking me away. "M'lady, don't! He's going mad with the fever! If ye must be here, git some fresh water. Quick! We must break the fever!"

Mindless of what I was doing, I whirled away from the bedside and made for the bathroom with the enamel wash basin she had plunged at me. I slopped cold water back to the sickbed, dipped one of the few remaining clean towels into the water and sponged his burning face with it. He didn't resist, but lay there very still, his mouth open as he gasped horribly for breath.

"That's the inflamm'tion of his throat and tongue. 'S not uncommon, m'lady, in severe cases."

"Severe cases?" I gasped, dipping my towel back into the bowl.

"The typhoid's made terr'ble progress with him, m'lady.

Usual'y the delirium don' set in so fast, and he's only been sick less than three days, too!''

He groaned mildly at the onslaught of the cool towel on his forehead. Glancing closer I saw that his skin had a sickening yellowish cast as if the film of sweat tinted it.

''He's burning up!'' I cried as I attempted to peel away the sodden shirt.

His limp arm was heavy, and I heaved my way underneath him to pull the shirt away. Rose was immediately next to me, holding his muscled torso while I pulled the shirt up and over his head. I flung it to the floor.

The linens under him were wet and stale from his loss of fluids. Rose laid a clean, wet cloth across his forehead. He groaned deeply and turned his head. A vein in his neck beat with an accelerated pulse, and his neck and face were flushed the color of a ripe tomato. His lips, dry and cracked, were swollen and white.

''Don't you think we should give him some water to drink?'' I asked with alarm.

''Don't know if he can keep it down. He's been wracked with stomach pain and wretchin'. I've tried to give him liquids, but he jus' sends it up again.''

Shaken to the core by his unexpectantly severe condition, I found a cup with fresh water and held it to his mouth.

Clutching the cup tightly, I forced his lips apart and poured some of the cool liquid down his throat. He sputtered and gasped, spitting some of the water out. But once he had swallowed the bulk of it, he fell back on his bed, muttering confusedly under his breath.

Once I saw that he kept the liquid down, I removed the rag from his forehead and rewet it.

''Give me some clean towels,'' I asked Rose over my shoulder.

''There ain't no more, m'lady. Used 'em all up, and I ain't had time to launder anythin'.''

I looked at the stained, smelly heap of linen on the floor. I had used the same towel repeatedly until it stank of sickness and was turning yellow from his sweat. I began removing my frock.

Rose looked at me in abhorrence. "M'lady! What'er doin?"

"I'm going to use my dress for towels, that's all," I answered as I unbuttoned the long row of buttons and stepped out of the plain gown.

It was a relief to remove my dress as the room was heavy with heat. Wearing only my silk petticoat over a lace-trimmed chemise and corset I began ripping the thin dress material into shreds. It was an old, ugly thing, anyway, and was best used for a purpose like this.

I scooped up my heavy hair from the back of my neck and mopped at my perspiration wetting my underarms and under my breasts. Fatigue gripped me as I spent the rest of the early evening at his bedside, wiping away the sweat that poured from him profusely. When I tried to remove the sodden linen, Rose warned me that there were no more clean sheets. I kept sponging him, hoping the typhoid spots on his backside didn't become ulcerated.

At one point during the evening Rose pulled open the drapes to reveal a pale blue sky with pinpricks of silver dotted against the velvety canvas. The fire was built high and it kept the room unbearably stuffy, but it was best to keep him warm—and sweating.

As the shadow of night fell upon us, Charles sunk into a dim delirium. He was rambling madly and thrashing his arms about. And when Rose went to the kitchen for another mustard plaster, he seemed to know I was in the room with him.

His eyes closed, his tongue thick with white fur, he lashed out with fury. "Damnit, girl! Get out. Get out now. Leave this place! He'll come for you!"

Desperate for him to sleep again, I mopped at his wet brow and made low murmurings of comfort. He seized my arm so fiercely I thought he would break it. Opening bloodshot eyes, he peered menacingly at me.

"Minnie! Don't get close to me, you'll catch the dratted sickness, don't"—his lids closed and he breathed heavily—"come close. I'll die, and then you'll . . ." He turned his head away and sunk into unconsciousness.

I gripped both of his strong arms, now lying limp as a babe's at his sides, and started weeping senselessly.

"You musn't die! You won't! I won't let you! Oh, Charles, I love you so much, really I do." The choking, drowning tears did nothing to assuage my pain, and when Rose returned I calmed myself and helped her apply the plaster to his rising sores.

He didn't yell out or try to stop us. His breathing was suddenly light and even, but the room smelled like death.

I fell back into one of the wing chairs and fanned myself with a scrap of cloth. "Well, how is he? He'll live, won't he?" I sat straighter and watched her. "Please, Rose, tell me he'll live!"

"I don' know, m'lady. Y'er case was so mild compared to his, and when my mother"—she grabbed up another piece of material, wetting it and rubbing down his face—"when my mother had the fever, she didn' git it so bad, neither. I don' know what to say, m'lady."

Heavyhearted, I moved slowly to the window and stared out at the night. But I didn't see anything; my every thought was for Charles. He must live! I prayed silently. He must! A tear rolled carelessly down my cheek, then another. I was so tired . . . and weak . . . and now I felt utterly despondent.

Suddenly the room spun around me in a dazzling jumble of leaping fire, heat and oppressive smells. Rose rushed to me and helped me into a chaise lounge opposite the bed, reprimanding me for being up in the first place. She hurried to the kitchen and soon returned with a bowl of the steaming broth, new bread from the oven and a cup of wine, all calculated to restore me.

While Charles lay without making a movement, I ate and drank and felt my ebbing energy return. Then I was able to convince Rose that since Charles's restlessness had abated I could stay with him while she got some sleep. Without much prodding, she left me.

I opened the window only a crack and breathed in the clean air. It was a warm evening; a heavy dampness hung on the night, but the air was mercifully fresh. I came back to the bed and lowered the cock on the flickering lamp at Charles's bedside table. A soft, wavering glow lit him.

I glanced at the chaise lounge. Would he be all right if I closed my eyes for a few minutes? I was so tired, and I would surely hear him if he called out for me. I lay down on my side, facing him, totally heedless that I was striped to my underclothes. And within moments I drifted off.

When I awoke a dull gray light was filtering into the room. I sat up with a start. I had slept all night! Nothing game me such a shock, however, as when I saw Charles was awake, his eyes dull and expressionless. He lifted his head slightly, but he didn't seem to see me. I wasn't sure if he was blind or still delirious! I'd heard hideous rumors that many who recovered from typhoid lost their eyesight.

I ran to him and he turned at the soft rustle of my petticoat.

"Charles! Are you awake! Can you see me?" I asked breathlessly.

Slowly, with great effort, he pulled a strong arm from under the quilt and held it out to me. I crouched next to him, eager for some response. He touched the skin of my neck and brushed his hand down my collarbone to where the ruffles of my chemise started. I didn't flinch or try to move away. His hand wavered there, flatly, against my warm skin, until he finally pulled away. He said in a gasp, "Dear . . . you're so lovely . . ." Then, dropping his hand, Charles fell once again into oblivion.

It was an interminable time before Charles showed any sign of recovery after that. Daily, as I tended him, my own strength increased. Though I slept little and took no exercise, my stamina was restored. My whole world was contained within the four walls of Charles's bedchamber. From Captain's Flynn's occasional visits, we got snatches of news about the camps and the men there. Luckily the epidemic hadn't spread into Duluth; it was confined to the miserable residents of Agate Bay, Tower and all those towns with Indian names. . . .

Doctor Clemens had recovered, it was rumored, but he suffered severe necrosis of his fingers and toes. There was no clue to the mysterious lady's whereabouts. Rose could tell me no more about her, and I had to be satisfied that I was out of danger . . . at least for the moment.

And no one appeared to have seen Francis.

I still wondered if *I* had even seen him plummet to his death—or if that had been only a terrible hallucination. But everything else that happened that day was etched vividly in my memory, and I had little doubt that I, alone, was witness to Francis's horrible end. . . .

One morning, after giving Charles some water and wrapping a clean quilt around him, I observed him closely. He was breathing deeply and rhythmically. Like a slumbering child.

I leaned over him and clutched his blankets, giving a silent prayer.

Suddenly his eyelids fluttered, and he moved his hand up from the blankets to touch me. He opened weary eyes and met my gaze.

"Dear, you've saved me . . . bless you." His voice was hoarse and barely audible.

I brushed the tears from my cheek and tried to speak without faltering. "Oh, Charles, you're going to be all right!" A thrill of hope raced through me. He would live! I realized—not for the first time—that I had never loved Clyde like I did Charles. My unreasonable ecstasy at his recovery was unlike anything I'd ever felt.

He lifted my hand to his lips and grazed a kiss there. I closed my eyes and inhaled. How intoxicating to feel his rough face against my skin!

"You're beautiful today, Minnie," he said thickly. My eyes flew open, and he stared at me with a lazy coolness. He turned up his lips in a sultry smile, showing his white, even teeth. "You're not becoming maudlin, are you, dear? Surely my illness was not as bad as that?"

I pulled my hands away and sat stiffly next to him. I had, indeed, become far too earnest. But whenever I was near him, my very being was infused with an all-consuming weakness and languor. Yet, even as I yearned for his touch, a sense of dark dread washed over me. This cannot be, I reproached myself. For who was this handsome, exciting man, really?

"You've been very ill, and I'm only concerned for your well-being," I said carefully.

"Ah! So cautious, are we, now? I thought you'd tossed out all restraint the night we danced around the fire," he said with scorn.

I felt the blood stain my cheeks at the mention of that last night together. "Oh, that—" I said glibly.

"Yes, that!" A shadow fell over his lean face. "I suppose it must seem inconsequential to you now that you've, no doubt, seen Francis recently."

I put my hand to my mouth in a breathless gasp.

His fathomless eyes became pure dun-gray, and his glance spelt danger. "Don't act so surprised, dear, though you really are quite a good actress. It's a wonder you left the stage at all, for any man!"

I stood and turned away from him, then walked over to a gleaming silver tray with plates of dry toast, marmalade, two boiled eggs and tepid coffee. I had to find something to do with my shaking hands.

I cleared my throat and said primly, "Oh, Rose brought a lovely tray for my breakfast. Has your appetite returned? Would you care for some toast with mar—"

"Don't be a fool." His voice was weak, but full of annoyance.

I turned. "What?"

"You know perfectly well what! I hope you at least had presence of mind to find out how soon he'll be paying me the forfeiture bond." He had pulled himself up and was now leaning on the pillows, watching me.

I poured a cup of coffee and brought it to him. "I said nothing to him." It shocked me how normal my voice sounded.

He refused the coffee with a shake of his head.

"I suppose that means you didn't speak about us, either?" he spat sarcastically.

I tried to recover. "I . . . I didn't speak to him about *anything* because I didn't see him! He never arrived," I said breathlessly.

"I see," he sighed, his powerful anger suddenly leashed.

"He . . . I went to the train station, and the guard informed me that someone had arrived and was looking for me."

If I didn't explain this part of my story, how credible would my tale be? For there were witnesses who had seen me swoon and almost faint. And, I assumed, Francis's luggage had arrived at the inn.

"And?"

Giving a sharp, artificial laugh, I said, "I tore out of the station looking for him, and I never saw him again." I avoided eye contact. "Never," I said in a whisper.

"Where do you suppose he went?" he queried, and I noticed how tired he had become. His habitually tanned face was wan; his cheeks were drawn under the shadow of his two-week-old beard.

"I . . . don't know. There was an awful storm that afternoon. Perhaps—"

His smile was depreciating. "I hardly think Francis was victim of the storm, if that's what you are suggesting!" He paused and ran a hand across his stubbly chin. "Have you reported him missing?"

"Missing?" I asked vaguely. "No, I didn't think it

necessary.'' I brushed at a tendrel of hair that had fallen loose from my chignon.

He glanced at me shrewdly. ''Minnie, what happened to him?''

I stared at him for a whirling moment. Somewhere in the depths of the rambling inn a clock struck eleven, then I heard the distant buzz of the servants' bell.

His eyes became heavy, as though he could barely keep them open. ''I suppose you must go,'' he sighed under his breath, mercifully giving up on his deadly inquiry.

''Yes . . . yes, I have to go help Rose now; you know we've no servants left! They all fled when I was brought home. I had the fever, too.''

He knit his brow with drowsy concern. ''I'm sorry, Minnie. So very sorry. . . .'' His voice was very weak.

''You must rest now, go back to sleep, Charles. You've been terribly ill.''

Abruptly I made for the door. The conversation had almost careened out of control, and I wanted to disappear from the room.

He said nothing, but turned his head slightly to watch me go. I quickly pulled the door closed behind me, wondering if I had just spent the last of my luck.

Chapter 15

The next morning life was as it should be. The outside world had not encroached upon us yet. Charles wakened and, fully rested, claimed to be ready to read his long-neglected mail. His renewed strength encouraged me, and I went about my morning routine cheerfully. I was not used to housekeeping tasks—nor did I enjoy them—but I delighted in the activity if only to keep my mind off what disasters might soon befall me.

When I brought him a clean, pressed shirt and trousers, he seemed mildly amused at my embarrassment. An hour later, after bathing, shaving and dressing, he made his slow descent to the main lobby and parlor.

Though he looked thinner, his physique still had a well-developed musculature that made it impossible for him to seem frail. Trying to contain my fervent delight at his renewed vigor, I went into the parlor ahead of him and was busily lighting the brass-mounted wall lamps when he entered.

I turned at the soft whisper of steps across the carpet.

"There's no need for you to work so hard, Minnie," he said rather crisply.

Whether he noticed that I wore a new lilac teagown, he didn't say, but his smoldering stare suggested that I looked pretty.

I pulled the tasseled cords on the drapes to reveal a warm, cloudless day. "Hardly," I answered just as tartly, "Rose has done most of the work to keep the inn together. But it seems as if the guests have all but disappeared." He was walking toward me, dangerously close. "Your railroad must be completed . . . ?"

He stood before me and looked down at me. Though I was nearly five foot three, he towered almost a foot above me.

"Yes, we've finished on time. As soon as I'm able, I will supervise the first delivery of ore to Agate Bay."

"You must be quite pleased," I said stiffly.

I was beginning to understand the heated declarations of the young man at the miners' camp. Was Charles ruthless in his determination to finish on time even with so many of his men ill or dying?

I played with a gold tassel on the drapes. "How did you do it when your camp was in the midst of a typhoid epidemic?"

To my pained surprise, he threw back his head and laughed. "So, that's what's eating you! It wasn't easy, dear, I assure you! I hired an extra thousand men and found several experienced cooks to feed them well. Fresh beer and water were brought in and slowly the fever abated. And the remaining tracks got built on time."

"Congratulations," I said.

"I detect that you don't mean those words," he said, his head back, a glint of white teeth showing.

I darted a furtive look at him, and he said abruptly, "Minnie! What are we going to do?" He reached round my waist, drawing me slowly to him. Without rational thought, I tipped my head to meet his, and his mouth pressed hotly on mine.

Neither of us exercised any measure of restraint. The deep desire, locked so carefully within us these past weeks, came pouring forth like a flood. His kiss was savage, fierce, cruelly selfish—anything but gentle. I delighted in his violent strength and let his strong arms engulf me. I was lost to the sensation of his caressing mouth when, suddenly, there came a stiffled gasp. I thought at first I had uttered a sound of ecstasy, but Charles released me swiftly, and I knew, with horror, that someone was in the room with us.

"I'm sorry to disturb . . ." I heard Rose's faltering voice before I leaned from my position trapped behind Charles to witness her. She was breathless and her face was flushed to the roots of her hair. I felt sorry for her embarrassment.

Charles was quick to recover himself. He walked to Rose, but I couldn't tell if he smiled, since his back was to me. When he spoke his voice was warm, however.

"It's difficult to resist the passions of one's beautiful wife after such a long illness," he said.

It was my turn to blush deeply. I was glad for their conversation, which prevented either of them from looking at me.

"I'm terribly sorry; it's only that yer door was open, and I—" Rose was speaking again.

"Oh, don't be ridiculous. No harm done. Please come in. And what do you have in your hands?"

"Two wires, sir! Come firs' thin' this mornin'. I jus' thought I better git 'em to ye right away."

"Yes, thank you, Miss Rose, I'm glad you thought to bring them quickly," he said, taking the telegrams.

Charles went to his writing desk and reached for his glasses. Placing them on his nose, he sat on the edge of the small, worn desk, and with one leg swinging, he perused the telegrams intently. Rose and I exchanged a quick, apprehensive look.

Slowly his gaze came up, and he turned to regard me intently through his spectacles. His eyes were dark and grim. How peculiarly like Francis was Charles in that stern moment! I darted a look at the telegrams that lay crumpled on his desk.

"It seems your sweetheart Francis is not so sweet after

all. According to the mayor's office in New York, he's going on trial for murder and it's my lawful duty to find him!''

I gasped and held onto a velvet armchair for support. Rose's bright blue eyes were as round as pennies as she gaped at Charles, then at me. She whispered ''sweetheart?'' but I couldn't answer.

''He was on his way to Minnesota over a month ago. Since then he hasn't turned up anywhere.'' His words were low and laced with anger.

''*Murder*?'' I exhaled finally. ''How could . . . what has he done?''

''I was thinking of asking you the same question,'' Charles shot back sarcastically.

Before either of us could utter another word, Rose burst out, ''Oh, m'lady! That's the name ye kep' callin' out in yer sleep! Ye kep' askin' for someone named Francis cause ye was worried if he was all right. You was 'fraid that he'd died in the storm.''

Charles watched Rose, then turned a deadly stare upon me.

''It doesn't surprise me that you called out for him, Minnie.'' The whiplash of his tone smarted. ''But what I want to know is why you lied and said you hadn't seen him when we both know perfectly well you did?''

I pulled a handkerchief from the lace trim at my sleeve and slid it nervously through my hands. ''I . . . I don't know. . . .'' I said lamely, then burst into tears.

A cardinal lit on the open sill and sang for a glorious moment before flitting away. Its joyous song seemed a cruel mockery to the oppressive silence in the room.

After Rose had rushed to me with a cup of cold water, my tears quickly abated. Her troubled face was alert and keen to our conversation, but she asked nothing. I sank into the deep cushions of the armchair and blew my nose.

''What do you mean you don't know?'' Charles had lowered his glasses. He remained perched on the edge of his desk, his eyes no longer sparkling dangerously. Instead he watched me with an open curiosity.

"It's just that . . . Oh, Charles, I was followed! He followed me—in the midst of the deadly storm—and I ran through the woods to the Witch Tree. . . ."

Rose gave a strangled cry.

"And then?" Charles's voice held the cut of steel in it.

"And then . . . he . . . he asked me . . . why I hadn't answered his letters," I lied. "Why I wasn't—"

"It was my understanding that you had been in correspondence with him," he said.

"No! I was too afraid. I was being watched—" I stopped myself. How much of my treacherous secret was I exposing?

"I don't remember why I didn't write him," I said weakly, kneading my wet handkerchief. "I only remember his fury. . . ."

"Yes," Charles looked away, smiling disparagingly. "His fury. I can well imagine." His eyes, cool and gray and contemptuous, came to rest on my face again.

"What did he say to you?"

". . . Only that I was wrong, that I—Oh! I don't know! I don't remember! I was too frightened." I began to cry again.

Charles shot me a quick, scornful glance. But his tone became a little gentler, as though he wanted me to continue unhindered.

"Fetch her a clean handkerchief, Rose," he said, and soon he was crouching at my side.

I accepted the lace square of cloth and wiped my eyes. He saw my hesitation and gently he prodded me to continue.

"Go on," he said softly while he watched me grapple with my emotions. "Maybe if I can know the truth now, there will be no secrets between us anymore."

I raised my shamed head and looked at him. Though his words were soft and encouraging, there was no message of forgiveness or compassion in his eyes, which wrenched my heart. He fixed me with his keen, steady gaze and let me continue.

"You see, the waves were lapping upon the rocks, and I was standing there, watching him . . . when he reached out in a rage for me as if he would throw me into . . . the water."

If I was disobeying my most earnest promise to myself by telling the story, I couldn't stop now. Charles stiffened, poised like an animal listening, while Rose retreated silently to a dark corner of the room as I recollected Francis's inglorious death.

"And as he lunged for me, his arms outstretched, he slipped. An enormous wave splashed ashore and took him with it. . . ." I said brokenly. "I watched for him to resurface, but there was no sight of him."

"The Devil's Kettle!" Rose announced.

"I suppose there's not much use searching the lake for him now I've heard your story. He must have drowned immediately," Charles said with deadly calm, rising to his feet.

"But I suppose we must contact the Coast Guard anyway. And the police. They'll all have to be notified." His voice held the chill of barely-contained anger in it.

I practically flung myself at Charles. Gripping his cream-colored trousers, I pleaded foolishly, "It'll be all right, won't it . . . ? Tell me that nothing will happen to us! You can drag the lake . . . try to search for his body, but, please, tell me that we'll stay together anyway. . . ."

He savagely gripped my hair and jerked my tear-stained face away from his legs, where I clung like a child.

"Look at me!" he said grimly.

Trying to contain myself, the tears running heedlessly down my face, I met his look.

"How is it you loved Francis so much that you came halfway across the country to marry his brother just so you could wait for him here? And now that's he dead all you're concerned with is whether you and I are going to be together?'' he demanded.

''*His brother*?'' I whispered on a sob.

I heard Rose's stiffled scream from the shadowy corner where she remained.

Charles narrowed his eyes and stared at me with suspicion. Abruptly he smiled, his lean face drawn up in a mirthful expression that contrasted with his pallid countenance.

''How thoroughly convincing you are! Sometimes I almost believe you had never seen Francis until the . . . night that he died! Don't worry,'' he said bitterly, pulling away from me. ''I won't let anyone in on your little secret. No one will ever suspect that you were with him when he died. That way they'll be no questions asked. Don't you agree, Rose?''

She answered with a stunned little cough, then managed to say ''Oh, yes . . . yes, sir. No one 'il niver know.''

He made for the coatrack and grabbed his bowler and suit coat. Tipping his hat graciously to us, he said, ''Now, ladies if you will excuse me, I have quite a large ordeal ahead of me.''

A long, shivering sigh went through me. ''Where are you going?'' I asked desperately.

He answered me slowly, deliberately. ''My dear, to the police. Then, when I have reported Francis missing—and most likely dead—I will send a telegraph to the poor, distraught mayor of New York informing him that the criminal Francis has been served justice. And after that . . . I will go to Agate Bay. To get my first shipload of ore ready to sail. And then, most likely, there will be a memorial service in New York for my deceased brother. Would you care to join me at the memorial service? I'm sure he would have wanted you to.''

His harsh words, his cutting voice, his expressionless face made my shame unbearable.

''No,'' I said raggedly. I couldn't say more.

He slowly answered my agonized look. ''I think I'm beginning to understand now.''

For a lethal moment his eyes held mine in a perilous gaze, as though he saw me for the first time. Then his words cut the silence. ''If you will pardon me while I attend to the distressing business.''

He moved away in an engulfing rage, unnecessarily slamming the door closed behind him. I stood, inflamed to a pitch of fright such as I had never before experienced. *What would become of me? How could I survive the dire future that would surely belong to me now?*

Chapter 16

For the next two weeks I tried to escape the painful, bottomless pull of grief. But my efforts were in vain. The heartache remained with me through my endless days of ordeal.

The inn began to come alive again with new guests. All the servants had returned, including Mrs. Svenson, and I welcomed the noisy intrusion of activity. Yet something off-key tugged at me still. It was the idea of Minnie marrying her sweetheart's *brother*!

". . . Marry his brother so you could wait for him here," Charles's deep voice echoed in my head.

Why would anyone marry their lover's brother . . . ? Unless the lovers couldn't be found out—unless it was morally wrong, unless one of them was married already. . . .

A man called Inspector Jackson, from the police office, accompanied Captain Flynn on the *Ella G. Stone*, but they could find no trace of Francis's body. The lake was searched several times, and the reports were sent to Charles, who had fled again to Agate Bay. It was said that he triumphantly supervised the first cargo of iron ore shipped to Cleveland, Ohio, before it continued to New York harbor. Charles hadn't bothered to communicate the good news to me himself.

In fact, he had communicated nothing. All that was left of

our relationship was the memory of flinging myself grievously at him. I was thankful that he had, indeed, stayed in Agate Bay, for my feelings were too vulnerable to be submitted to Charles's scornful gaze again.

Daily I worked on two new dresses that I had designed. They would go with me when I left—for I must certainly leave. This time for good. But there would be no hurried note thrown under his door. I would tell him good-bye in person at least—when my courage returned.

And I would let him know I couldn't return to New York again, where only painful memories existed for me. . . .

One evening at the end of September when the air held the chill of autumn, Rose knocked at my door. I sat comfortably in my window seat netting a purse.

We had hardly spoken at all since that day with Charles, and I know she was desperate with worry for me—and him. But propriety held her tongue, and I, fearful of what truth might be revealed if I talked too much, said nothing. As she moved cautiously into the room, holding something dark that caught a gleam of light, I could see that her anxious expression had not changed.

"M'lady! I found the bottle!" she said under her breath as if someone might be listening.

"The bottle?" I looked up.

"The bottle a' Old Blacky, m'lady."

I practically leaped out of my seat, dropping my stretch of net to the floor.

"Where did you find it? I thought that woman took the bottle with her?" I gasped, rushing to her.

"So did I. But it seems she just tried gittin' rid of it by stashin' it in the coal bins, where one a' the men found it."

"One of the manservants found it?"

"Yes, m'lady, jus' yesterday mornin'," she said, holding the container out to me.

"But what I come t' tell ye is not *where* I found it, but *what's* in it!"

"You *know* what's in it?" I asked incredulously.

"Yesterday was my day off, y'know, so I went t' town lookin' for Dr. Clemens. He's lookin' mighty poor I mus' say! Anyway, he checked over this tonic for me."

"And what did he say?"

"He sniffed it and even tasted the tiny drop that was left, and as he choked, he looked at me and says, 'Who was drinkin' this, Miss Rose?' and I says back, 'My mistress at the inn got it fed to her durin' the fever.' And do know what he says?"

"No," I said with alarm.

"That yer mistress is lucky to be alive!"

"What is it made of?" I asked in a gravelly voice.

"Pure opium steeped in saffron, cloves and a certain type of pow'rful acid."

I set my jaw and glanced at the worn label: LANCASHIRE GENUINE BLACK DROP. "Rose, has this woman truly left this time? You see, she's . . . she's been after me . . . she wants my life!"

Rose flung her hands to her cheeks. "Oh, m'lady, you don't mean it!"

I said in a voice as thin as paper, "I wish I didn't mean it . . . but nonetheless I'm her victim . . . as long as she is on the premises."

Rose shot me a pointed look of inquiry, but asked nothing.

I invited Rose to stay for tea and cake because I wanted her company, but also I wanted to find out if the mysterious woman had, indeed, gone.

"She's gone, m'lady! I didn't see her, but cook saw her board the landau and drive away!" Rose nervously informed me.

What I couldn't fathom was why the mysterious lady had, indeed, fled when Charles returned to the inn with the fever? Wouldn't she have wanted to stay near her lover? Her inexplicable disappearance worried me since she had left so many times before. Only to return again. I could only hope the reprieve from my terror would be permanent this time.

For I wasn't quite prepared to leave the inn . . . not yet anyway.

One bright autumn afternoon, several days after my conversation with Rose, I got the news that Charles had finally returned from the camps. My rising anxiety was given a focus, and I summoned Rose to find out how soon Charles could see me. Then I dressed carefully in a nut-brown and gold gown newly created from lengths of velvet. I styled my hair in a neat chignon and added a faint dot of rouge. When Rose came back I was happy to learn that Charles would see me immediately in his suite.

I knocked softly on his door and didn't expect him to open it so suddenly. I tried to hide the tremor of excitement that raced through my body as I quickly took him in. He was still dressed in his wilderness costume—tight knee breeches that revealed perfect, muscular legs, mud-splattered Hessian boots and a heavy, close-fitting shirt that displayed the magnificent breadth of his chest. The skin on his face and corded neck had lost its pallor; he was browned again by the sun. His look grazed my velvet dress, but he said nothing.

I rushed past him, my skirts whirling around my legs, and tried to summon all the courage I could.

"I've been waiting for this meeting," I blurted out defensively.

He moved carelessly in front of the hot, red light of the dying fire. For a moment only a faceless, dark silhouette loomed up before me. Then he moved to one side, placing an arm on the mantel and smiling lazily.

"And it seems you've been dreading it as much as I have," he said casually.

"It's understandable," I said lamely. "They haven't found Francis's body yet, have they?" It was more a statement than a query, for I knew that he had not been found.

"No, I'm afraid not." He crossed the room and pulled a book from the wall of shelves. His back was to me when he spoke again. "I just spoke to Captain Flynn, and he said the chances of finding his body are very slim."

A shudder raced through me. He turned abruptly and looked at me. The soft glow of gas, the plush furniture and brocade drapes all disappeared, and suddenly he was a ship's captain from the Renaissance, wearing a red coat and ruff, leaning on starboard waving good-bye. Nothing else mattered but the two of us lost in that suspended moment.

"I'm not surprised. After all, according to you, he went down at the Devil's Kettle by the Witch Tree."

I forced a smile. "Surely you don't believe all the old wives' tales about objects being sucked under never to return?"

"No, I don't. But I do believe that there is a whirlpool at work there that causes certain things to disappear. As I've said before there is a space around the Witch Tree that is held sacred, and I think that is where this whirlpool is located. Just about every object that falls in there is sunk." He tossed the book on the settee and shoved his hands in his pockets, looking away.

Objects such as human bodies, I thought morbidly. "Only the evil . . ."

"Yes," he said, his dark eyes meeting mine again. "Only the evil are drowned."

I stared at the swirl of muted colors in the carpet.

"Minnie," he said, in a voice suddenly cold, "there will be a memorial service for Francis held next week in New York. I don't suppose anyone has contacted you since no one knows of your involvement with him, so I will do the asking. Will you accompany me back East? You will come as my wife, of course, to save face."

"I see," I said evenly. His unexpected question threw me out of gear, though I'd often thought about this dilemma in the long days while I waited for Charles's return.

"What . . . what good would it possibly do for me to be there?"

His raised his eyebrows arrogantly. "I don't know. It's

your choice. I only thought you'd want to pay him your last respects."

I floundered. "Yes, I . . . I do. But not there. Not in front of . . . anyone else," I lied foolishly.

His gaze did not waver from my face. "Then, let's just call it even. I'll escort you back to New York, anyway, and you can pick up your life where you left off."

I made a shallow, coughing sound. "That's what I came to see you about. You see, I'd prefer not . . . to go back. I think I might like to stay in the Middle West. Take a position somewhere. . . ."

He shot me a glance, half-scowling, half-surprised, and didn't answer.

"You see, I have no money of my own and I—" How much was I revealing?

"Yes, it's doubtful that Francis would have left you much in the way of income," he said matter-of-factly.

His words crushed my last hope. I, who had greedily accepted Minnie's offer as a chance to live well, was poor again.

"I would only like to ask if I may stay long enough to find employment?"

To my surprise, he threw back his head and laughed without rancor, showing a glint of white teeth.

"You don't have to ask my permission to do anything. You haven't up to this point, and I have no idea why you feel the need now! Nevertheless, you may stay and find a job. But I can't imagine who in this vast plain is going to have much need of a Broadway actress. Unless, of course, you are an accomplished singer, then you can hire out for the social functions of the wealthy."

His amusement sparked my indignation. "I don't see how my dire situation is humorous. But it doesn't matter what you think anyway, I suppose." I was losing footing and tried not to let my anger carry me away.

"I don't think it will take me long to procure a position, and then I'll be out of your hair forever," I said levelly.

While he watched me his smile faded and a stormy bleakness settled upon his features.

"Please, I apologize for any insult I may have made you. Do you think I would leave you to fend for yourself entirely? Without my setting you up with an income?"

Pitiful as my finances were, I could not accept money from Charles. I must be strict with myself now. There could be no ties that bind. . . .

"No, Charles, there is no need to set up an income for me. I can easily find work."

"Nevertheless, I feel there is a need, and I will arrange something with my accountant as soon as possible." He held me sternly with his eyes, and I knew there would be no more mention of money. I cleared my throat and looked away.

"I will pack and go alone to New York. There is the nasty business of Francis's trial that I will have to contend with, anyway. I will clean up all the paperwork, close our business arrangements, and, of course, you are free to go at any time."

"Thank you," I replied shortly.

There was quick pause before he spoke again.

"God knows what political entanglements Francis had." He picked up an old brass microscope and twirled the ivory handle. "Murder! I believe it!"

The image of that ruthless, inexorable face rose me before again.

"So do I," I whispered.

Glancing at the wall behind him I noticed the space where Renoir's portrait of the girl had been. My heart was wrenched at the thought of the lovely gift.

Without warning he moved to the door and leaned against the wall to let me know the interview was over.

I didn't hesitate. Moving swiftly, the heels of my satin shoes making quiet brushing sounds against the rugs, I was as eager to be out of his presence as he was for me to leave.

As I made for the doorknob, he reached out and grabbed

my wrist firmly. I didn't resist his grasp, but looked up at him. His face was a sculptured mask, cold and unfeeling, and a new rush of distress washed over me.

"I'm sorry," he said in a raspy undertone.

"For what?" I queried nervously, feeling the world fall about my hapless head.

He ignored my question. His eyes were faraway, stern-browed and bitter, as if he watched a distant memory lost now to time. He loosened his hold on my arm and let it drop.

"If you haven't found work by the time I return, perhaps we will see each other again." His eyes came to rest on my face once more.

"Perhaps," I said. I managed a tremulous smile and said, "Then good-bye." But my quivering voice must have given me away.

"Good-bye," he said evenly.

Looking away, I managed to take my leave without his seeing the burning, ugly tears that had already begun to fall.

Chapter 17

The pounding on my bedroom door was insistent.

"Madam! Mrs. Whitney! There is someone here from the police office that insists on seeing you!" I recognized the voice as Mrs. Svenson's and pulled myself out of my dreamless slumber.

Sleep had not come easily to me last night because I had just found a position with a newly rich family in St. Paul as a lady's seamstress. I would start the job as soon as I was able to pack my things and get there. The terrible dread of knowing I would leave Charles forever tormented me until, after a fit of weeping, I had given up the struggle and fallen asleep.

"Come in," I said wearily.

The doorknob shook and rattled. "Madam! It's locked!"

Her voice held the shrill note of alarm, and I wondered why she was so surprised that I had locked the door last night. I locked the door all the time now . . . yet hadn't it upset me, too, when I first discovered I would have to lock myself in at night?

"I'm coming," I announced drowsily as I pulled a cotton robe over my thin nightgown.

I shivered. Autumn had little time to linger, for the cold breath of winter was in the air already. My fire had not been lit, and around the curtains peeped a dull, gray light. It must be early.

I opened the door to a stern-faced Mrs. Svenson. She gathered up her ruffled skirts and came hurrying into the room.

She glanced around. "Where is that girl? Hummmph! No fire lit and it's near to eight o'clock!"

"Oh my. I have so much to do today!" My comment was something between a reminder to myself and an exasperated remark to Mrs. Svenson. No one knew of my plans to leave yet.

"I can imagine," Mrs. Svenson returned glibly. "But before you do anything, madam, an Inspector Jackson from the police and Captain Flynn are here to see you."

I glanced at her for a fervid moment.

"What do they want?"

"Oh fiddle! They wouldn't say. So I put 'em in the parlor with a nice cup of tea and some of cook's raisin buns. They seemed content with that. And I told them I'd have you come right down. I didn't know you'd slept so late."

"I'll be right there," I said in a hushed voice, trying to marshal my rocketing fears.

Mrs. Svenson sensed the uneasiness that gripped me and changed her tune. She suggested that I not let my agitation get the better of me, and that I should take my time with my toilet. I agreed with her, but when Mrs. Svenson left me to dress, her face was pulled in an exaggerated affectation of worry.

I wasted no time in pulling myself together. After washing, I dressed in an orchid silk-and-cashmere teagown, plaited my hair, pulled a new *visite* over my shoulders to ward off the chill and pulled on my winter satin heels.

I was aware, as I moved along the closed, gloom-infested hallway, of impending disaster. The inn had a dank, corrupted atmosphere all of a sudden, and I knew, before my feet hit the bottom step in the foyer, what had happened. Francis's body had been found, and in Charles's absence—

Charles had been in New York for over a week now—I would be called upon to identify Francis.

I couldn't do that, I thought. I'd hardly had a chance to see him that dreadful day, and to gaze upon that sinister face again would surely be too horrible.

The color in my cheeks rose as I entered the warm, cheerful parlor. A table had been prepared, laid with sparkling china and cutlery. The soothing aroma of camomile tea and fresh-baked rolls assaulted me, making me aware of my empty stomach. The two bearded men were silent as they took their refreshment. At the sight of me they rose immediately and removed their hats.

"Mrs. Whitney," they said in unison.

"Thank you for coming to see us at such short notice," Captain Flynn said with a forced smile, bowing gallantly while he held his hat in front of him. "Please allow me to make introductions."

I was seated at the crimson-covered table and offered a cup of tea, which I accepted gratefully. Mr. Jackson and I exchanged strained pleasantries, which I resented, so anxious was I to hear his news. When I tipped the china cup to my lips it quivered, and I realized that I was actually trembling.

"Please, gentlemen, tell me what brings you here?" If they wouldn't get to the point, then I would do so myself.

The inspector cleared his throat. "Yes," he said, leaning back in his chair, his index finger hooked in his vest pocket.

I strained forward in keen anticipation. My heart stopped; I held my breath and bit my lip. "*You've found the body*?" I exhaled almost without sound.

The inspector looked surprised, almost shocked. Captain Flynn turned white.

"We were both jolted by it, I can certainly say." The men exchanged a quick, scandalized glance before the inspector continued.

"Mrs. Whitney, a body has been found. But not the body

we were looking for. Not the body of Francis Whitney, your brother-in-law. We found the body of a young woman."

I gulped for breath and dropped the dainty cup in its saucer with a clack! I was stunned into a senseless stupor. For a moment the world was a whirling, incomprehensible place.

"*Woman*?" I finally gasped. "Where . . . where . . . did you find her . . . the body?"

The captain wiped his mouth carefully on the linen napkin. He laid it next to his plate with deliberation before he spoke.

"On a shoal north of here. Her body was washed upon the sandbar, and the inspector here can't be certain how long she had been there. You see, she has begun to decompose. . . ."

His voice trailed off. The only sound in the room was the low tick of the bracket clock above the mantel. I'd never even heard it before above the normal daily sounds that permeated the room. For no particular reason I glanced at Charles's empty, narrow desk. It was bare except for the emerald oil lamp.

"Have you identified her?" I asked without feeling, although for some reason I felt certain I knew the answer. Charles's lover had died. He would never see her again. . . .

The inspector fidgeted with his cup. "We'd hope to ask you to do that for us. We assumed that she was related in some way to either you or Mr. Whitney by the necklace she still wore."

"What do you mean?" I asked dully.

Unexpectedly the chintz wallpaper, Turkish carpets, mahogany furniture and the concerned men that sat before me all seemed to belong to some reality that was lost to me. Too many wicked twists had been thrown into my path, and suddenly I was glad to be leaving.

The inspector was talking again. ". . . It is a lovely thing, really. I have it right here."

From his suit coat he pulled a neat white handkerchief and unwrapped it gently. A diamond locket poured out from the cloth and fell heavily upon the table. I leaned close to examine it, then I reeled back and gasped. It was the one from Francis!

The inspector ignored my agitation. He pointed a thick finger toward the bottom of the locket.

"See here . . . the name Whitney in gold letters around the bottom."

"Madam?" the captain asked, "do you know this necklace?"

"Yes . . . yes, it belongs to his . . . to Charles's mother, I believe." My utterance must have sounded false, but it was the only story I could think of.

"Then this woman is related to you, or rather, to your husband's family?"

"I believe so . . . but I don't know," I answered vaguely.

"Since Mr. Whitney is still out of town, we can only turn to you for assistance. We can think of no one else who might know who this woman is. Can we spare a moment of your time today or tomorrow to come to the county morgue to identify the . . . this woman?"

I stood and turned away from the men. I faced the door and stared out at the hallway, where I heard the murmurings of male voices.

"I don't think I'll be able to do that, gentlemen. I wouldn't know her. I've met none of my husband's relatives."

"I see," came the captain's reply. His voice was lowered then, and he obviously spoke to the inspector.

"It's strange . . . the woman must have come from this area. Have you ever thought that, perhaps, she doesn't belong to the Whitney family, even though she was wearing an obvious family heirloom?"

The inspector only grunted. The captain's next question was directed at me again.

"Mrs. Whitney, was any jewelry sold to strangers that you know of?"

"It's possible," I said half-turning, glancing in the direction of the open door.

Charles stepped slowly into the room. He was back and much earlier than I'd expected! He must have made a concerted effort to have returned in less than a fortnight. My disbelieving stare was riveted to him as he flung his coat, hat and cane upon the coatrack, then removed his gloves, pulling at each finger while our eyes held. He tossed them on the rack, too, and I was enthralled by his sophisticated dress. He wore a navy reefer with a stylish soft-fronted shirt and a crisp, white collar.

"Gentlemen, Mrs. Whitney," he said with a hint of smile.

"Hello," I said softly.

The men moved forward eagerly and they shook hands all around. There was a rush of talk. "You're back just in time, Mr. Whitney . . ." and "Your lovely wife has been good enough . . ." "Someone has been found," and "a body?" "Yes, a woman's body and we have reason to believe she is a member of your family. . . ."

Charles went to the table and glimpsed the necklace lying there.

How unbearable it became for me to stand there, wringing my hands as I watched Charles scrutinize the necklace. He held it in his hands for a moment, then turned to me.

His eyes held the question that he never asked. I could only stand there foolishly watching him, wondering what to do next.

Inspector Jackson shot me a bewildered look. "Is it the necklace that belonged to your deceased mother?" he asked Charles.

Charles wavered a moment before answering. "Yes. It was my mother's."

Not for the first time was I reminded how truly I loved Charles. Though he spoke evenly, his words carefully measured, I knew, with some sixth sense, that he did all this for me. It is impossible to explain how I understood in that moment that he cared for me, too. But something in his concerned manner alerted me. He kept darting glances aimed in my direction, and when the conversation headed toward identifying the body again, he insisted on doing that alone. This woman was most probably no one that I would know, he claimed, and it was nothing that I should be asked to do. He was certain he knew who she was, anyway.

The anxious men took their leave as Charles assured them he would come to the morgue later that day. He closed the door behind them.

I stood ardently watching him, afraid of what I might say if I spoke.

He walked to the fireplace . . . dangerously close to me. "Minnie, I made a terrible discovery in New York."

My ears burned. He had distractedly picked up a ceramic figurine from the mantel and was touching its smooth surface.

"I discovered why Francis was wanted for murder."

I said nothing but watched him with dawning fear.

"There was a political conspiracy against him!" He smiled disdainfully. "I should have known that he'd get into trouble with that rough bunch of cutthroats!"

"Yes," I said hollowly. What group had Francis been involved with?

"Supposedly he had a violent dispute with Boss Kelly over who should run for mayor. All the Tammany members thought there was a real need to depose Mayor Grace—you know, the steamship tycoon. Kelly called Grace an ingrate and was eager to get a strong candidate in the running. Francis wanted a strong candidate, too, but he had a different man in mind. You know how stubborn and driven Francis was!" he said glancing at me.

I nodded silently.

"Well, it seems Francis wanted a certain Hugh Grant to run. He was rich, affable and seemingly honest. It was said he didn't accept bribes! But Kelly wouldn't allow Grant in the running. There was a lot of heat between the two men. One morning Francis and Jimmy the Famous—you know, one of Kelly's men—started arguing about the election candidates. They started fistfighting, and before long one thing led to another. It seems they drew guns and, in the midst of their heated debate, Francis shot his opponent in the chest. Jimmy died later that night."

"Ohhh!" I shuddered, putting my hand to my mouth. What did all this really mean?

Charles set the figurine back on the mantel, then picked up a poker and dug into the barely glowing embers of the fire. A half-burned log fell with a hiss! and the fire sparked a moment.

"You can only imagine the ramifications. Kelly was hot on Francis's trail. No wonder Francis decided to come and visit you when he did. He had to escape—he was to be tried for murder by the grand jury!"

"But wasn't it really an accident?" I asked, hoping that Minnie really hadn't fallen in love with a murderer.

"If you mean that Francis had no intentions of actually killing that man, yes it was an accident. But I can't help thinking that no matter what had happened, Francis was putting his trust in the wrong place, dealing with the wrong men." He passed a hand over his face.

"Yes, it would seem so!" I said mindlessly.

"And the wrong women!" he said with barely leashed anger.

"Women?" I cried.

"That dead body in the morgue . . . I know who she is."

I felt myself begin to go limp, and I could hardly manage to keep standing.

"I'm not surprised that she stole your necklace, either."

I gasped and sat down on the settee in front of the fire. "*What do you mean*?"

"Last June, just after you arrived, Francis had his first

disagreement with Kelly. Kelly, as you know, didn't get his coveted position by being soft-hearted and forgiving. He's vicious and extremely dangerous, and when he decides not to trust someone, that person's life is in great peril. Anyway, Kelly decided to keep a close watch on Francis. He discovered that Francis had a mistress—you, of course. . . ."

Yes, me, I thought with uneasiness.

". . . So he hired Francis' ex-whore, sorry, darling, but she was a prostitute, you know, to come back here and taunt you. To find any incriminating evidence—you know, letters between you and him, even some of my papers were missing. She took everything she could get her hands on. She was out for revenge. This proof of his affair with you would be shown to Francis's wife, of course, and the story sold to every rag in New York. This Madame Renee Cousteau hated you, hated Francis's wife, too, but I think she hated you more because she knew Francis was in love with you. You see, she was still in love with him herself."

My lips were dry and my heart was going wild. *Francis's wife*!

"And in the process she frightened you, threatened your very life. I've no doubt that she was behind the sudden collapse of the footbridge."

"Oh, Charles!" I gasped.

The woman, the evil, horrible woman, was *not* Charles's lover but Francis's jealous ex-lover! That I'd almost died at her hands seemed to make no difference now that I'd learned the truth.

I played with the lace ends of my *visite*, trying to keep my threatening tears at bay. The little clock whirred and struck ten.

"I was so enraged and . . . scared for you. I had an appointment with Kelly himself and told him that if one hair, a single hair, on your head was injured before I returned to the inn, I would kill him with my own hands. I caught the first train home." His voice was tight and faraway.

Gulping down a new onslaught of tears, I stood. "This Madame Cousteau . . . is the one in the morgue?"

"Yes, I've no doubt about it. It doesn't surprise me that she is wearing the necklace of yours that was a gift from Francis."

I felt his eyes on me though I looked down.

"I'm sorry any of this ever happened," he blurted out, and suddenly, as though a mist lifted, I saw clearly, for the first time since my arrival at the inn.

Charles was a lonely figure, fighting against the dictates of a world not of his making. He didn't fight back with his fists like his brother did, he fought with his intellect. His battle against convention brought him to this frontier, where he discovered he could make a fortune shipping iron ore East. But not without ready cash to set himself up. So Charles went to the source he knew would have funds—his brother Francis, who was in the thick of New York's political underworld. In return, Charles had to marry Francis's mistress and take care of her until Francis could divorce his wife. Charles had taken a bride—sight unseen!

He came to me then and pulled me into his arms. His touch, his kiss, his eyes told me everything. And yet . . . I couldn't believe it. Could he really feel this passion?

"I love you," he murmured into my hair. "I love you so much . . ." His raspy voice trailed off and he began kissing me again, almost with desperation. It was as though he really needed me now!

He led me back to the settee and held me in his arms for a long while. He was no longer stormy and bitter, as he was when I last saw him. He was tender and passionate and full of forgiveness. I sat woodenly in his arms, afraid to allow myself to give in to the longing that I'd felt since I'd first seen him. I could not allow myself to make any more mistakes, I thought as he hotly nuzzled my neck, murmuring my name. I had been so impetuous when I had flung myself at him not so very long ago—how could I be sure this time?

Slowly he pulled away, holding my hands with his own,

and looked at me darkly. ‘‘It’s too late for us, isn’t it?’’ he asked abruptly.

My numbness surrendered to a surge of emotion that I was unable to control. The blood rushed into my head and my pulse began beating with a drum’s insistence. I clasped his hands tighter in my own, but didn’t answer.

‘‘Have you found a position?’’ he asked.

‘‘Yes . . . I have. It’s with a certain Hill family in St. Paul. They’re—’’

‘‘I see,’’ he said swiftly. He rose and went to the mantel again and watched a dying spark of the fire. ‘‘Minnie, if you want to go, I won’t stop you. I’ve set up a nice income for you, and with that you should be able to live comfortably without work if you choose.’’

‘‘Oh, I couldn’t!’’ I resisted.

He held up a hand. ‘‘Let me finish. But if you want something different . . .’’ He faltered and became guarded. ‘‘Minnie, I have a question for you.’’ He lifted his head but didn’t look at me.

‘‘Yes?’’ I whispered.

‘‘Now that Francis is gone, it seems there is nothing holding us back, doesn’t it? Except our own fears.’’ He turned then and faced me.

‘‘I would like you to stay with me. To live with me as my wife. My real wife.’’

Quickly I went to him and put my arms around him. ‘‘It’s not too late. It’s not too late!’’ I breathed against his shirt. My throat was so full I was barely able to whisper the words.

We held each other for a long moment before he said with a faint tremor in his voice, ‘‘Then you will stay with me? Be my wife and put all the past behind you? Because I love you more than you’ll ever know. I really do . . .’’

‘‘I love you, too, Charles. I’ve always loved you from the first moment. I’ve never stopped.’’

He loosened his hold and looked down at my face. A

pained smile creased his mouth. "That doesn't say much for Francis, does it?"

"Oh, Francis!" I said on a rush. "Charles . . . there's something you must know. Francis means nothing to me; I've never met him before. I'm someone else! I'm not Minnie at all, but Minnie's cousin, Maggie, come here to design dresses for her!" Revealing my true identity was the release of a tremendous burden, and I felt suddenly giddy.

He smiled lazily down at me and it was spring again. "I'm so glad," he said carelessly. "I would hate to think that I had stolen my brother's woman . . . even if it is fair!"

I laughed mirthfully.

"So you were telling us the truth about your identity after all?"

"Of course I was! How could you believe I wasn't?"

He laughed this time. A gay, spirited chuckle, and he drew me into his arms again.

"Ah, my love, that's something you will never understand since you never knew Francis."

"But I—"

"Shhh!" he said suddenly, placing a finger to my lips. "It doesn't matter anymore. All that matters is you and I. The world be damned!"

I was held in such a cocoon of happiness that I couldn't argue.

He looked at me, and I knew that he belonged to me as he never could before. Somehow I got it into my stubborn head that he really loved me and needed me. We talked about what we would do with our lives, about how we might travel, visit Egypt or Spain or Italy, where the hot Mediterranean sun would renew our spirits. Where we could laugh and forget the past.

Full of fresh optimism for the bright future I had yearned for once before but had not gotten, I let Charles go so he could attend to the grisly task he must face in town.

Grabbing his hat and coat and cane, he turned to me, his eyes gleaming with passion.

"While I'm in town I'll purchase two tickets for a steamer to Europe. It'll be our honeymoon!" And he was gone.

I clasped my hands together and sank into one of the plush chairs. For no reason I noticed how the waxen whiteness of my wrist contrasted with the orchid cuff of my gown. A skittish sun peeped out from its cloud cover and infused the room with autumn's orange glow. Thrilling to the warmth and golden peacefulness surrounding me, I heard Minnie's voice filter down to me in the words of an old proverb, "All that glitters is not gold."

A bittersweet melancholy rolled over me. I would miss her, and I wished I could thank her for her role in my fate.

A loud knock at the door brought me reeling to my senses. I jumped up and pulled it open without delay.

At first the man standing before me made no impact. He was an elderly gentleman with old-fashioned gray fringe whiskers and silver-rimmed spectacles. Dressed in a black traveling suit, he looked rather dignified, and I thought at first he was a colleague of Charles. Before I could tell him that Charles was not at home, the old man smiled warmly. And I recognized him. It was my next-door neighbor from New York.

"Maggie Mansfield!" he said.

Chapter 18

An autumn mist lingered, settling upon the colorful leaves strewn across the road. As I puffed my cheeks out impatiently, I could see my breath in the damp air. It was over an hour and still he had not come. I hugged my *visite* warmly to me when my ears became aware of a distant thunder.

Suddenly the sound of galloping hoofs echoed through the trees and Charles came into sight, his coat flying out behind him. I was reminded of that first time he had surprised me on his horse, and I wondered if he would look at me the way he did that day. . . .

Abruptly he reined in his horse to a prancing halt. He glanced at me quickly, and before I knew what was happening, he reached down with a swift, smooth motion, lifting me up behind him on his mount. I held on tightly as we tore ahead into the woods, past the beautiful, haunting stretch of sugar maple, yellow birch and pine. The ocher sky was fathomless, and soon I heard the roar of the surf. We were close to the shore and the point of land where the Witch Tree was indomitably perched.

At the sudden end of the woodlands, Charles halted the horse and we both dismounted. He grabbed my hand and led me down that rocky course that led straight for the Witch Tree. The water had a dull, glassy sheen as low, rolling waves hit the rocks at the foot of the tree. With a rush of anxiety, I stiffened.

"Come," he chided. "Don't be afraid. The Witch Tree only takes the lives of those who are evil."

"Yes," I whispered. But after seeing Francis's terrible death those old wives' tales no longer seemed foolish.

Charles leaned against the twisted tree and reached for me. I let him caress my face, my neck, my hair. I closed my eyes and listened to the gray-green breakers rush timelessly against the shore.

"Maggie . . ."

Though he knew my name now, the sound of it startled me, and I looked at him. He grazed his thumb across my cheek and watched me without smiling.

"I met your neighbor in town, and he told me that your former husband died in a fire in your stables recently."

"My God! You know already!" my voice was clutched, tight, as if the sound stuck in my throat.

"Yes, I know," Charles answered gently.

I looked out at the restless water, trying to marshal my rioting emotions. My shock of hearing of Clyde's death had been tremendous. My grief had burst forth like a flame, then, miraculously, it had died just as suddenly. Now I was only relieved. For I had already suffered great despair at the dissolution of the marriage.

"When I first saw my neighbor at the inn, I was so frightened . . . I knew something had happened to Clyde. Something awful."

"I'm sorry." His eyes were sad for me.

"I . . . I hadn't told you about my marriage because I wasn't sure I wanted you to know—not yet anyway. But when I heard the news . . . somehow I felt suddenly closer to you." My voice was a bare whisper above the water. "I even waited on the road for over an hour to catch you coming from town. I wanted to tell you everything myself."

"Divorce is not a sin, no matter what you may think," he said evenly.

I smiled. "My neighbor said he'd been searching for months trying to find where I'd run to. The . . . fire in the stables happened at the end of June."

"Just after you arrived at Witch Tree Inn," he said carefully.

"Imagine! Traveling all this way to give me the news that Clyde had died over four months ago! I guess no matter what role I played the world was still there to intrude! I'm only glad my neighbor had a sister to visit in St. Paul."

We both stared at the moving water. Then he said, "Your neighbor also said that your divorce was completely understandable, given the circumstances." Charles's voice was thick and unsteady.

"Yes," I said.

Charles was grave-faced. "Tell me about him . . . about your ex-husband."

"Clyde Mansfield—once a famous actor."

"Yes, I've heard of him. But what was he really like?"

There was a pause as the great tide sprayed ashore.

"He . . . he came from scrambling beginnings on the Lower East Side. And he was always bitter about his past, bitter because he was forced to earn an income. He thought he should have been born a Vanderbilt or Astor. He spent money wildly, and when the debts started getting bad, he sank into despair. And never gave up the anger that plagued him."

I put my hand to where his thumb touched my neck and held it there.

"I wouldn't doubt that his death was suicide."

"His bleak unhappiness stole yours, didn't it?"

"Yes . . . yes, oh, how I wanted to be happy! Even if we were poor I could have survived it, but to be poor and unhappy! It was too much to bear. Especially since I never knew if my husband even loved me. . . ."

"I'm sure he did." Charles's voice was soft as velvet.

I made no reply, but felt his muscular hand against my skin and noticed the pale blue glow of Minnie's sapphire ring on my finger. How strange that I would know so little about this handsome stranger with the brooding brow who touched me so tenderly! Yet in that instant it mattered little that his past was as cloudy as the distant shore. I knew him as he was today and would be in the future . . . when all the lies and subterfuge would be forgotten.

I looked at him, suddenly remembering that he had just returned from town, from his terrible errand. Spurred by morbid curiosity I changed the subject.

"And did you . . . could you identify the woman?"

He shuddered and pulled away. "It was difficult. Her body was badly decomposed . . . but it had to be Madame Cousteau."

"She must have died right after you arrived at the inn with the fever. I wonder what happened."

"Does it matter? They're all gone. All of them. Now even their ghosts can't haunt us. We're too invincible for them. Don't you agree, Mrs. Whitney?"

I smiled through the tears that clouded my eyes.

A great black-and-white bird swooped menacingly low, trying to get back into his nest in the old tree.

"You know, she hid letters in the tree. Do you suppose her offerings were meant to make peace?"

"Perhaps . . . or perhaps she merely wanted to hide the letters until she could safely pack them away and get back East."

"Yes, I suppose. . . ." I reached my hand around Charles to feel the craggy bark. "Somehow I feel that the tree knows our suffering and feels it, too. It has withstood so many setbacks and still it grows, its roots knotted around the rocks, like an old, patient hand."

Charles laughed and pulled me to him. "You are a poet, my dear! With an imagination to go with it." He looked into my eyes and tilted my chin to him.

The washed-out light touched his face, and a wavy lock of hair fell over his dark forehead. "I've purchased the tickets to Europe that I promised you," he said softly.

"I'm so glad!"

But nothing made me as happy as living right in that moment, knowing Charles was mine forever.

"And I was thinking how you might like having your own home, so I've arranged for some rather clever architects from Chicago to make some preliminary sketches for us."

A home. I would have a home!

"Oh, Charles!" I began, but words were impossible now.

"Let's try marriage the proper way this time," he said and kissed me as he had never kissed me before.

Suddenly we were alone in the world, alone in that great wilderness, and I felt that no one would ever hurt me again. The low sky touched the distant shore in a deep gray that looked cold as the coming winter. I could endure all my winters now.

Languishing in Charles's arms, I heard Minnie's haughty laughter. It only manifested itself out of my subconscious, but it was real, nonetheless.

" 'Love is familiar. Love is a devil. There is no evil angel but Love!' It's a line from Shakespeare, darling, and I'd recommend not forgetting it!"

I won't forget it, Minnie, not if I live for a hundred years. . . .

Postscript

Before my true identity could be properly restored, it was arranged that Dr. Clemens give me a thorough examination. After which he attributed my switched identity to a malady known as "railway spine"—a psychic condition that was known to appear after a traumatic shock.

At first Dr. Clemens had thought I was healthy. He'd assumed that I was, indeed, Minnie and there was nothing more to it. To discover that I was really Maggie made Dr. Clemens highly agitated, and the whole town, in fact, whispered about me. He said he now realized that I had been suffering a mild psychopathological disorder.

And four months later, on the eve of our honeymoon, I officially became Maggie again.

I smiled ironically at the doctor's diagnosis. The name on the death certificate had to be changed, of course. As well as the name on the wedding certificate.

"A consummate storyteller."

—Mary Higgins Clark

BARBARA MICHAELS

NEW YORK TIMES BESTSELLING
AUTHOR OF
SOMEONE IN THE HOUSE
AND *INTO THE DARKNESS*

BE SURE TO READ BARBARA MICHAELS' BESTSELLERS

__INTO THE DARKNESS 0-425-12892-X/$5.50
__PRINCE OF DARKNESS 0-425-10853-8/$3.95
__THE CRYING CHILD 0-425-11584-4/$4.95
__SOMEONE IN THE HOUSE 0-425-11389-2/$4.95
__SEARCH THE SHADOWS 0-425-11183-0/$5.50
__SHATTERED SILK 0-425-10476-1/$5.50
__BE BURIED IN THE RAIN 0-425-09634-3/$4.95
__AMMIE, COME HOME 0-425-09949-0/$4.99
__SMOKE AND MIRRORS 0-425-11911-4/$4.95
__WAIT FOR WHAT WILL COME 0-425-12005-8/$3.95
__WINGS OF THE FALCON 0-425-11045-1/$4.99
__SONS OF THE WOLF 0-425-11687-5/$4.95
__THE SEA KING'S DAUGHTER 0-425-11306-X/$4.99
__THE DARK ON THE OTHER SIDE 0-425-10928-3/$4.50

For Visa, MasterCard and American Express orders ($10 minimum) call: 1-800-631-8571

FOR MAIL ORDERS: CHECK BOOK(S). FILL OUT COUPON. SEND TO:

BERKLEY PUBLISHING GROUP
390 Murray Hill Pkwy., Dept. B
East Rutherford, NJ 07073

NAME____________________
ADDRESS____________________
CITY____________________
STATE__________ ZIP__________

PLEASE ALLOW 6 WEEKS FOR DELIVERY.
PRICES ARE SUBJECT TO CHANGE WITHOUT NOTICE.

POSTAGE AND HANDLING:
$1.50 for one book, 50¢ for each additional. Do not exceed $4.50.

BOOK TOTAL $____
POSTAGE & HANDLING $____
APPLICABLE SALES TAX $____
(CA, NJ, NY, PA)
TOTAL AMOUNT DUE $____

PAYABLE IN US FUNDS.
(No cash orders accepted.)

"A moving love story...the perfect mix of tenderness and adventure."

—Jill Marie Landis, bestselling author of *Jade*

NORMANDALE COMMUNITY COLLEGE
LIBRARY
9700 FRANCE AVENUE SOUTH
BLOOMINGTON, MN 55431-4399

SEA OF DREAMS

Elizabeth DeLancey

Two hearts on a journey of desire...

Norah Paige must leave with her employer on a six-month voyage across the Atlantic. Parting with everything she holds dear, Norah boards the ship and hesitantly embarks on her journey . . .

But the ship is captained by Rob McKenzie, a man she once knew—and secretly loved. When Norah steps back into his life, he's seduced by her tenderness and charm. Norah's life is transformed, until a bitter truth threatens to tear them apart—and put an end to their love forever . . .

___*1-55773-681-2/$4.99*

For Visa, MasterCard and American Express orders ($10 minimum) call: 1-800-631-8571

FOR MAIL ORDERS: CHECK BOOK(S). FILL OUT COUPON. SEND TO:

BERKLEY PUBLISHING GROUP
390 Murray Hill Pkwy., Dept. B
East Rutherford, NJ 07073

NAME ____________________

ADDRESS ____________________

CITY ____________________

STATE __________ ZIP __________

PLEASE ALLOW 6 WEEKS FOR DELIVERY.
PRICES ARE SUBJECT TO CHANGE WITHOUT NOTICE.

POSTAGE AND HANDLING:
$1.50 for one book, 50¢ for each additional. Do not exceed $4.50.

BOOK TOTAL $ ____

POSTAGE & HANDLING $ ____

APPLICABLE SALES TAX $ ____
(CA, NJ, NY, PA)

TOTAL AMOUNT DUE $ ____

PAYABLE IN US FUNDS.
(No cash orders accepted.)

393